KITTY in the
CANDY HEARTS

KITTY in the CANDY HEARTS

Ben M. Baglio

Illustrations by Ann Baum

Cover illustration by
Mary Ann Lasher

AN
APPLE
PAPERBACK

SCHOLASTIC INC.

New York Toronto London Auckland Sydney
Mexico City New Delhi Hong Kong Buenos Aires

ISBN 10: 0-439-87119-0
ISBN 13: 978-0-439-87119-8

Text copyright © 2007 by Working Partners Limited.
Created by Working Partners Limited, London W6 0QT.
Illustrations copyright © 2007 by Ann Baum.

12 11 10 9 8 7 6 5 4 3 2 1   7 8 9 10 11 12/0

Printed in the U.S.A.   40
First Scholastic printing, January 2007

Special thanks to Andrea Abbott

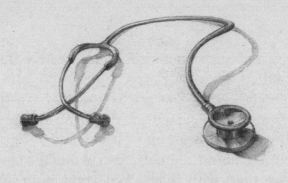

One

"*Corny?*" Mandy echoed in dismay. "What do you mean, corny?"

James Hunter stared at the poster lying on the kitchen table. Mandy had glued an enormous red foil heart in the middle of a sheet of black cardboard. Beneath this, she had written in large gold letters, WE LOVE YOUR PETS! Next to that, she'd drawn a girl hugging a kitten and a puppy, and sketched a heart-shaped goldfish bowl with some smiling fish in it.

James took a deep breath. "Well, Valentine's Day is about romance and things like that. You know, *human* stuff. It's not an animal thing."

"There's nothing wrong with saying we love animals," Mandy said.

"Everybody knows you do. You don't have to spell it out. Or *draw* it." James sat down at the table and pulled the poster toward him. "If you and your parents weren't crazy about animals, you wouldn't spend all your spare time with them. And your mom and dad wouldn't be vets."

"I guess not," Mandy said. "And Animal Ark wouldn't be part of our home." She could never quite get over how lucky she was, living in a house with a veterinary surgery attached!

"Exactly! A poster like this . . ." James touched the shimmering foil heart and made a face, ". . . is kind of, well, overstating it, don't you think?"

Mandy wrinkled her nose. "You really think so?"

James nodded. "But I still think you should put it up in the reception area."

"What? You just said it's corny and that animals and Valentine's Day don't go together. Make up your mind."

"It's corny the way it is," said James. "So we'll change it."

"How?"

"Like this." Bending over the poster, James began to write something in pencil below Mandy's sentence about loving pets.

Mandy read the words out loud. "*And — worms — do — too!*" She burst out laughing. "That's perfect! This is exactly the right time of year to remind owners about deworming their pets!"

James blushed. "I'm glad you like it."

Mandy watched while he drew an ugly-looking worm with huge sharklike teeth. He finished it off with another sentence. MAKE SURE YOU DEWORM YOUR PETS — EVEN YOUR GOLDFISH — REGULARLY!

Mandy traced over his sentences with the gold pen. When she'd finished, they took the poster through to the reception area of Animal Ark. As they went in, Mandy glimpsed a brown tail disappearing into her mom's treatment room before the door closed behind it. She looked forward to seeing who the patient was.

Jean Knox, the receptionist, looked at Mandy and James over the top of her eyeglasses. She pointed to the poster in James's hands. "Another lost pet?"

Whenever a pet was missing or a stray was found, Mandy and James put posters up everywhere. They'd had a lot of success with finding pets new homes — there was barely a house in Welford, the Yorkshire village where the Hopes lived, that hadn't taken in one of their stray puppies or kittens!

"Not this time," Mandy said, dragging a chair to the wall opposite Jean's desk. She climbed onto it, and

James handed her the poster. Using Sticky Tac, she pressed the four corners firmly against the wall. She looked over her shoulder at Jean. "What do you think?"

"A Valentine's greeting for pets? What's next, Mandy Hope?" Jean read on and smiled. "Hmmm, I see what you're getting at now. I'd better make sure we have enough deworming medication in stock."

Mandy jumped down from the chair just as a woman and a young girl came in. The woman was tall and thin with short black hair. The girl was tall, too, and probably about Mandy's age. She had shoulder-length auburn hair and a dusting of freckles on her cheeks.

Mandy didn't recognize them, so she glanced at James to see if he knew them. He shook his head.

The girl was carrying a wicker carrier. A mournful *meow* announced there was a cat inside.

"Hi," Mandy said. She smiled as another yowl came from the carrier. "Someone's not very happy about being here."

"Sorry he's making so much noise," said the girl.

"Don't worry about that. Most cats make a fuss when they come to the vet," Mandy told her. "They probably associate the smell of disinfectant with being handled by strangers or stuck with a needle." She went over to the girl and peered in through the wire door at one end of the carrier. The cat inside was a lovely chocolate

brown color and, judging by his size, still a kitten. He was squashed up against the side, his face turned away from Mandy.

Over at the desk, the woman was talking to Jean. "I'm Alexis Arquette. I called yesterday about our kitten."

"Ah, yes," said Jean, looking at the open appointment book on her desk. She picked up a clipboard. "Would you mind filling in this new-patient form please, Mrs. Arquette?"

From the carrier, there came another loud meow. Mrs. Arquette turned around. "Why don't you go and sit down, India? Todd might feel better if he's not being jiggled around."

India went to sit on a chair against the wall, below the Valentine poster. Mandy thought she looked almost as nervous as her kitten. She hoped there wasn't anything seriously wrong with Todd. At least there was nothing wrong with his voice!

Mandy went over to sit next to her. "India's a cool name," she said, hoping to help her take her mind off her cat for a minute.

"It's unusual," India agreed. "Mom and Dad went traveling before I was born. India was their favorite country."

James sat down on the other side of her. "Good

thing they didn't like Turkey the best!" he said with a grin.

India laughed. "Turkey Arquette! What a mouthful."

Todd interrupted them with another loud meow. "Sssh, Todd. Be a good boy," said India. "We'll go home as soon as you've seen the vet."

There was a sudden outburst from Jean. "Oh, goodness!"

Mandy saw her staring in bewilderment at the computer screen. "What happened?" she asked.

"I have no idea," Jean replied, frowning. "The spreadsheet I was working on has vanished and an empty one has taken its place." She looked closer at the screen, as if she expected to find the lost document that way. "Modern technology. It gives you nothing but headaches!"

"I might be able to figure it out," said James, going behind the desk. He looked at the screen for a second, and Mandy saw him click the mouse.

"There it is!" said Jean. "Where was it?"

"You had two documents open at the same time," James explained. "You must have clicked on the empty one so that it came up in front of the real spreadsheet."

"How on earth did I do that?" asked Jean, still looking baffled.

"Like this," said James, and he swiveled the mouse on the desk. "All you have to do is click here on the task bar to bring back a document."

"Oh, I see," said Jean, although from the puzzled edge to her voice, Mandy wasn't too sure that Jean *did* see. "Thank you very much, James," Jean continued. "I'd better make a note of this." She opened a small black book where she wrote down computer tips she'd learned from James.

"Another computer crisis avoided," Mandy said, winking at James as he came back.

"Hardly a crisis," he said, sitting next to India again.

India looked impressed. "Do you know a lot about computers?"

"A little," he answered. "They're one of my hobbies."

"My dad works with computers," said India, her green eyes lighting up. "He designs web sites."

"That must be such a cool job," said James. "I'd love to do something like that one day."

"He could show you how to," said India. "My dad's really nice. He gave me Todd, you know."

"That *is* nice," Mandy said, looking through the wire door again. Todd had wriggled around so that he had his back to her. All Mandy could see was a rounded brown shape and a tail swishing from side to side. "How long have you had him?"

"Since just before Christmas. He's thirteen weeks old now."

Mandy winced. She hoped Todd hadn't been a Christmas present. All too often, animals that were presents ended up being ignored by their owners when the novelty wore off. Mandy caught James's eye. He shook his head slightly as if he'd guessed what she was thinking, and was warning her not to say anything.

"Want to really see him?" India began to undo one of the buckles on the straps that held the door shut. "He's a pedigree chocolate-point Burmese. His real name is Haberay Algernon Todd."

Mrs. Arquette turned around. "No, India. Don't open the door. Todd might get out."

India stopped. "I was just going to show him to Mandy and James. I wouldn't let him escape."

Her mom raised her eyebrows. "Hmm. I've heard that before."

"That was different," India protested.

"That's enough, India," warned Mrs. Arquette.

The unexpected tension between India and her mom made Mandy feel a little uncomfortable. James looked embarrassed, too; he picked up a magazine and studied the cover closely. He couldn't have been interested in it, though. The magazine was called *Knitter's World*.

India ignored her mom's warning. "Dad and I were just getting him used to the living room —" She broke off as the door to one of the treatment rooms burst open and the dog, whose tail Mandy had glimpsed earlier, rushed out, dragging its elderly owner behind it.

It was a sturdy-looking dog, about the size of a Labrador. Mandy's first impression was that it was a cross between a Staffordshire bull terrier and a boxer. It seemed very strong because its owner was clinging to the leash as if his life depended on it. "Thanks, Dr. Emily," he said over his shoulder as he stumbled after his dog.

The frantic animal came to the sliding door and found his way blocked. Desperate to get out, he stood up against the glass and scratched at it.

Mandy ran to help. But by the time she reached the door the man had already slid it open. The dog shot out like an arrow from a crossbow. His owner tore after him. "I'll just get Muttley in the car, then come back and pay the bill!" he called back.

"I don't think he'll be putting Muttley in the car," said James, chuckling. "Muttley will put himself in."

"And he'll drag his owner in behind him," Mandy said, watching the dog pull the man across the lawn. She closed the door. When she turned around she saw that India looked upset. Her arm was around Todd's basket as if she was shielding him from whatever it was that had upset the dog. "Don't worry," Mandy quickly reassured her. "Mom wouldn't hurt Muttley."

Jean was looking over the top of her glasses at the dog and his owner getting into the car. "What exactly did you do to that animal, Emily?" she asked Mandy's mom, who had followed them more slowly out of the treatment room.

Dr. Emily Hope opened her eyes wide. "I checked his ears, that's all. But you know Muttley — perfectly reasonable until you lift him onto a table. Maybe he has acrophobia."

"Whataphobia?" asked James.

"Acrophobia," said Mrs. Arquette. She pronounced the word slowly, breaking it into syllables. "It means fear of heights."

"Oh. Right," said James.

"My mom's a teacher," India explained. "She's taking over as principal at the elementary school after this semester. English is her best subject."

Mrs. Hope had picked up a file from Jean's desk. "Todd Arquette?"

India stood up and brought the carrier across to Dr. Emily.

"So Todd's been a little sick?" asked Dr. Emily, glancing through the notes in the file.

"Yes. He coughed up something that looked like cardboard —" India began, but her mom took over.

"We're a little worried that he might have caught something after moving to a new area. He didn't do anything like this in our old house."

"Let's have a look at him then," said Dr. Emily. She stood to one side of the door and gestured to Mrs. Arquette and India to go into the treatment room.

"Can Mandy and James come in, too?" India asked. "I bet Todd would like to meet them."

"Sure," said Dr. Emily.

When everyone was inside and the door closed, Mandy's mom opened the carrier. She lifted the Burmese kitten out and put him on the table.

Mandy fell in love with Todd at once. Even though he was only three months old, he was one of the most elegant cats she'd ever seen. His body was long and slender, and his face was broad between the eyes and tapered to his chin, reminding Mandy of a Siamese cat. And just like a Siamese, his ears were big and pointed and darker at the tips. "He's absolutely gorgeous!" Mandy said, putting her hand out to stroke him. His coat felt like the finest silk. It was thick, and the exact color of milk chocolate.

The kitten purred loudly. He turned his head up to Mandy, his eyes closed with pleasure. "Does that feel good?" Mandy asked.

Todd opened his eyes. Their color took Mandy's breath away. "They're like pure gold!"

"He's certainly a magnificent animal. Friendly, too," said Dr. Emily, as the kitten rubbed his face against her hand.

"Mmm. But he's also a little troublemaker at times. And he can be very annoying. You should see the things he gets into," said Mrs. Arquette.

Mandy saw India roll her eyes.

Dr. Emily picked up her stethoscope from the table. Todd reacted with lightning speed. He lashed out with one paw and grabbed the instrument, hooking his claws in the rubber tubing. Then he began to chew it as if it was some tasty prey.

"See what I mean?" said Mrs. Arquette.

"He doesn't seem that sick," said James.

"He looks fine now," India's mom agreed. "Still, it doesn't hurt to have him checked out."

India was carefully unhooking Todd's claws from the stethoscope. "Bad boy. That's not yours."

"It's all right," said Dr. Emily, smiling. "Kittens can't resist going after things that move. And Burmese cats are known for being particularly playful." She eased the stethoscope away from the kitten. "I'll take that, thank you, Todd. Mandy, would you hold him, please?"

There was a special way of holding cats while they

were being examined, something Mandy had learned years ago. She took the loose skin at the back of Todd's neck in one hand, while holding his front paws with the other. "It's OK," she said, seeing India's startled look. She must have thought Mandy was being too rough. "I'm not hurting him. It's just like when a mother cat holds a kitten by the scruff of its neck."

Dr. Emily gave Todd a thorough checkup. "Temperature's normal. Mouth and ears fine." She felt his tummy, and listened to his heart and breathing. "Is he eating well?"

India nodded.

"Has he been sick before?" asked Dr. Emily.

"Just once, on the day after we moved here," said India. "It looked like he'd been eating a tissue."

Dr. Emily removed the stethoscope from her ears. "No digestive upsets as far as I can tell. He's as fit as a fiddle."

Mandy had pretty much expected to hear this. Todd was so lively he was the picture of good health. Still, it was good to hear her mom confirm this. India seemed reassured, too. She smiled at Mandy.

"No sign of any infection," Dr. Emily continued. "He probably just ate something that didn't agree with him. Keep an eye on him, though. If he gets sick again, bring him in and I'll run some tests."

Back in the reception area, Mandy and James waited with India while Mrs. Arquette paid the bill. India sat down again with Todd's carrier on her lap. This time, the kitten peered out through the wire door. Mandy rolled up a pamphlet about vaccinations and pushed one end through the wire, wriggling it in front of Todd who grabbed it immediately.

"You're really lucky to have him," said James.

"I know," India agreed. "I've always wanted a kitten of my own." She lowered her voice. "But my mom thinks he's annoying most of the time."

"What about your dad?" asked James.

India stared down at Todd's basket. "He likes Todd, but he doesn't live with us right now."

"You mean, he's away working?" James guessed.

India shook her head. "He still lives in York. He decided to stay there when Mom took the job here."

There was an awkward silence.

Luckily, Mrs. Arquette turned around just then and noticed Mandy's poster. "Oh! Deworming medication. I almost forgot."

Mandy grinned. "The poster's working, James!"

"It's a very clever reminder," said Mrs. Arquette. She turned back to Jean and took some money out of her purse. "How many pills will Todd need?"

"Just half of one," said Jean, putting a small white pill

in a plastic bag. "So keep the other half for the next time he's due."

Mrs. Arquette put the tablet into her bag. "Right. India, let's head home. We've got a lot to do."

Just before she reached the door, India looked back at Mandy and James. "Would you like to come and visit us?"

"I'd love to," Mandy said.

"How about tomorrow morning?" India suggested.

Before Mandy could answer, Mrs. Arquette cleared her throat. "Um, tomorrow's not a good day. We're going to buy new curtains."

India frowned. "The curtains can wait, can't they? They're not that important."

Mrs. Arquette raised her eyebrows. "You thought so yesterday when you were complaining that your room looked bare."

Mandy started to feel uncomfortable again. Next to her, James looked down at the floor, rubbing the toe of his shoe on an invisible stain.

"That was yesterday," India shot back. "And anyway, I thought you'd be happy for Todd and me to have some new friends."

"I am," said Mrs. Arquette. Her expression softened. "I guess we could go shopping later. You're right, friends are much more important than curtains." She smiled at Mandy and James. "We'll see you both in the morning, OK?"

"We'll be there," Mandy promised, relieved that the tension between India and her mom seemed to be over. And she could hardly wait to see Todd again, especially in his own home.

Two

That afternoon, Mandy went with her mom on her rounds to some farms outside town. It was a few weeks before the lambing season, and Dr. Emily was checking that all the ewes were in good shape. Mandy loved going on visits like these. It was a chance for her to meet up with some old friends — human as well as animal.

"While we're out, let's pop in to see Lydia," Dr. Emily said as they drove away from Graystones Farm, the last one on the rounds.

Lydia Fawcett lived at High Cross Farm with her herd of British Alpine goats. She sold goat's milk to local stores, as well as products made from it, like hand lotion, soap, and cheese.

"I want to buy something to send to Auntie Pip for her birthday," said Mandy's mom as they drove up the overgrown road to the farm. "I'll get some for Mrs. Arquette, too, as a welcome gift to go with your dish for Todd."

The ceramic dish was one Mandy had made in pottery class at school. It was yellow, and decorated with blue paw prints. Mandy had kept it for someone special. Having met Todd yesterday, she'd decided he should have it! Her mom had told her that India's parents had separated and were probably going to get divorced, so Mandy figured India could do with a warm welcome to Welford.

Lydia's farm was perched high on a hill, surrounded by stunted hawthorn bushes that sheltered the place from the icy northeast wind in winter. Not many people found their way up to the isolated farm, but today there was a white van parked in the driveway in front of the old stone farmhouse.

"Lydia's got company," Mandy said.

"Ernie, no doubt," said Dr. Emily.

Ernie Bell was Lydia's fiancé. He was a retired carpenter who lived in a small house behind the Fox and

Goose with his gray kitten, Tiddles, and Sammy, a gray squirrel. He had proposed to Lydia after a mix-up with an anonymous Valentine's card that had been delivered to the farm. At first sight they *seemed* an odd couple. Lydia had lived alone ever since her father had died and hardly ever ventured from the farm. Sometimes Mandy thought she preferred the company of her goats to that of humans!

Still, Mandy was sure Ernie and Lydia were perfectly suited. Ernie didn't really like being around lots of people, either. They could both seem rather gruff and short-tempered, but deep down, they had hearts of gold.

"I wonder how the wedding plans are going?" Mandy said to her mom. "I don't think anyone's gotten an invitation yet. And Lydia's hasn't said anything about her dress."

"Well, don't expect to hear anything today," said Dr. Emily, pulling up next to Ernie's van. "I can't imagine the two of them going for a big white wedding. It wouldn't even surprise me if they chose to get married here."

"That way the goats could be part of it, too," Mandy said. Lydia's wedding probably wouldn't be complete if her beloved goats weren't included in some way.

She jumped down from the Land Rover, squeezing in beside the white van. It was definitely Ernie's, but she hardly recognized it. It was a lot better looking than it used to be. "Ernie must have kept his promise to fix it up," she said.

When Ernie had proposed to Lydia she had agreed on condition that the spluttery old van was repaired. Instead of being dull and dirty, with dented fenders and doors and a sheet of crumpled plastic replacing the passenger window, the van looked like new. It was freshly painted, and Mandy couldn't see a single dent in the body. Seeing that the passenger window had been replaced as well, she added, "And Lydia can even ride in it without getting wet now!"

When Mandy knocked on the door of the farmhouse, there was no answer.

"They're probably bottling the milk," said Dr. Emily. The goats were milked early in the morning, and late in the afternoon. "I'll see if they're in the dairy."

"And I'll visit the goats," Mandy said, heading for the barn.

Inside the barn, the unmistakable aroma of goats and a chorus of eager bleating greeted her. "Hi, guys," she called. She started down the straw-strewn walkway between the two rows of pens. At each stall, she stopped to pat the goats and say a few words to them. They all had unique personalities, and Mandy knew most of them by name: Jemima, Lady Jayne, Monty, Olivia, and

Alexandra. If Mandy was asked to admit to having a favorite, it would have to be Houdini, a big billy goat as black as tar, with a strong straight back, a deep chest, and fine legs. He was smart and mischievous, and full of fun. And, like his famous namesake, quite an escape artist.

When Mandy reached his pen, it was empty. *I hope he hasn't escaped again*, Mandy thought. She and James had led Houdini back home on more than one occasion after he'd gotten out and ended up in trouble somewhere. *Maybe Lydia let him out into a field. It's not very cold today. I'll check after I've visited the others.*

She hurried on down the walkway, saying hello to the rest of the herd. In the last stall, a tall brown-and-white nanny goat named Olivia gave an excited bleat when Mandy looked in at her.

Mandy ran her hand down the bridge of her nose. "Is everything OK with you, Olivia?"

The goat tugged at Mandy's sweater with her big yellow teeth.

"No, Olivia. That's not food." Mandy picked up a handful of hay and offered it to her instead.

Olivia let go of the sweater and folded her rubbery lips around the hay. She munched on it noisily, her mouth working from side to side.

"You look like you're chewing gum." Mandy grinned and bent down to pick up some more hay.

Olivia sniffed Mandy's short blond hair. Stalks of half-chewed hay stuck out of her mouth and tickled Mandy's neck. "Thanks, but that's enough goat kisses for one day." She smiled, gently pushing the goat away.

Just then, a loud *clang* rang out from the far end of the barn, and Mandy spotted something moving in the shadows. "Houdini?" she called.

"No, Ernie," came the reply, and a small, wiry man appeared from behind a stack of hay bales. He was carrying a ladder under his arm and a can in one hand, and he was wearing baggy, paint-splattered overalls.

"Sorry," Mandy said. "I thought it was Houdini getting into mischief again."

"He'd better not be," said Ernie. He leaned the ladder against the wall. "I'm treating all the wood in here. It's been neglected for so many years it's splintering and peeling. It's a big job and I don't need that goat undoing all my hard work."

"I'm sure he won't," Mandy said. "Where is Houdini, anyway?" she asked.

"In his pen," said Ernie. "At least he *was*, ten minutes ago."

"He isn't now," Mandy said.

A yell from outside interrupted them. "Houdini!" It was Lydia, and she didn't sound very happy.

"I wonder what he's done this time?" Mandy said.

"I hate to think," said Ernie, raising his bushy white eyebrows.

They dashed outside, Ernie still carrying the paint can. Lydia and Dr. Emily were in the driveway with Houdini. Lydia was holding the billy goat by the collar and Mandy's mom was prying something out of his mouth.

"I'll take that, thank you, Houdini," said Dr. Emily, and she held the object up. It looked like a stick. But when Mandy got closer, she saw what it was.

"A windshield wiper!" She looked at the Land Rover. Both wipers were still intact.

"Well, I'll be . . ." Ernie was staring at the van's windshield. There was just one wiper on it, and it was sticking straight out. It looked like someone had pulled it out to wash the windshield.

Ernie glared at Houdini. "You rascal."

Houdini looked back at Ernie; Mandy could have sworn he was grinning.

Lydia started to chuckle, too. "He's impossible, isn't he?" She shook her head. "But at least we can get another wiper."

"Yeah," agreed Ernie. There was a hint of a smile on his lined face. "But there'll never be another Houdini."

"You'd have thought Houdini did it on purpose. Like he was playing a practical joke on Ernie," Mandy said, bicycling alongside James the next morning.

They were on their way to see India and Todd. It was a bright, frosty day, and the winter sunshine made the ice sparkle like jewels.

India and her mom lived in a neat stone house that was in back of the school's sports fields. Across the fields was the single-story redbrick building where Mandy had first gone to school. "It seems like a million years since I was there," she said. After leaving grade school, Mandy, who was now twelve, had gone on to middle school in Walton, a few miles from Welford.

They got off their bikes and pushed them up the sidewalk to the front door. Mandy leaned her bike against the wall and took the bag containing the gifts off the handlebars. She was about to ring the doorbell when she heard India and Mrs. Arquette talking loudly inside.

"There isn't enough closet space in my room," said India.

"Then you'll just have to get rid of some of your stuff, or put things away more neatly," said her mother.

"Everything *is* neat," said India. "And I already left a lot of stuff at home."

"*This* is your home, India," said her mother.

Mandy and James exchanged an embarrassed look. "It sounds like they're having an argument. What should we do, James?"

"Ring the bell, I guess." He pressed it. "They know we're coming."

The angry voices stopped immediately. Moments later, the door opened. "Hello, Mandy and James," said Mrs. Arquette. She was smiling as if nothing had happened. "Thank you for coming over. India and Todd could do with some company."

In the hall, India was sitting at the bottom of the stairs, glowering.

"Cheer up, India," said her mom.

India rolled her eyes. "It's not that easy."

Mandy swallowed uncomfortably. It was so embarrassing to find yourself smack in the middle of other people's arguments. Hoping to lighten the mood, she took out the gifts. "My mom sent you a present," she said, and gave Mrs. Arquette the gift-wrapped bottle of lotion.

"That's very kind of her." Mrs. Arquette unwrapped the present and read the label. It was in Lydia's beautiful copperplate handwriting. "'HIGH CROSS HAND LOTION. MADE FROM PURE GOAT'S MILK.' How lovely!"

"This is for you, India," Mandy said, giving her the other present. "Or should I say, for Todd?"

When India tore off the wrapping paper and saw the paw-patterned bowl she smiled. "This is so cute! Thanks a ton, Mandy. Todd will love it."

"Why don't you show Mandy and James your room while I make some hot chocolate?" suggested Mrs. Arquette.

India led the way upstairs. She still seemed a little quiet. But the moment she opened the door and Todd's tiny face appeared in the gap, her whole face changed. "There's my little angel," she said, laughing.

He looked up at her with his huge golden eyes and tried to worm his way through the gap. India quickly picked him up. "Oh no, you don't! Mom will have a fit if you go charging downstairs. And we don't want you getting lost."

"Hello again, Todd," Mandy said, stroking the kitten as he squirmed out of India's arms and scrambled up onto her shoulder.

"Mandy brought you a present," said India and she opened the door wider to go in. "Oh no!" She came to an abrupt stop.

"What is it?" Mandy looked over India's shoulder.

The room had been ransacked. The bedside lamp was lying on the floor, its pink shade crushed. There were bits of tissues everywhere, like flakes of snow. The almost empty tissue box was on the bed, next to a poster of a pop star. The poster was so badly shredded, Mandy couldn't tell who the singer was. And, to top it all, there was a big hole in a satin cushion that was lying on the floor.

"Todd!" cried India.

Even Mandy was shocked by how much damage the kitten had done. "It's like you had a party in here," she said, tapping Todd's nose with her finger.

"More like a riot," said James, looking around at the mess.

They went in and closed the door behind them. India put Todd down and picked up the cushion to look closer at the hole. "We'd better start cleaning up," Mandy said. "It's probably not as bad as it looks," she added.

"No, it's worse," said India.

Mandy took the cushion from her. "I'll ask my Grandma if she can mend it. She's good at sewing."

"Thanks," said India. "My mom hates sewing. And I'm hopeless at it."

James was kneeling on the floor next to the lamp. "I don't think we can do anything about the lampshade. I'll try, but it's really crushed. At least the base isn't broken." He put it back on the bedside table. "Let's see if it still works." He switched it on. The bulb didn't light up. "Probably just needs a new one," he said, unscrewing the bulb.

Mandy and India started to pick up the pieces of tissue from the carpet. Todd obviously thought it was a great game; he raced around, pouncing on the tissues and sometimes on Mandy's or India's hands.

"You're not helping, Todd," said India. She sat down on her bed and picked a few pieces of tissue off the bedspread. Todd scrambled up onto her lap and she pet him. He rolled onto his back and batted her hands with his little front paws. "You're a bad boy," India scolded him. "I wanted my room to be perfect for when Dad comes to see us."

"When's he coming?" said James.

"On Valentine's Day. He says he's bringing some things I left at home. But I think he's really coming to see Mom."

"To see if she's managing with the new house and everything?" Mandy asked.

"No, because of Valentine's Day. I mean, he could come any other day, so why choose then? And he's staying for dinner. So it's got to mean something," said India.

"Really?" Mandy said, glancing at James who was trying to smooth out the creases in the lampshade. He didn't return the look. Perhaps he didn't want to get caught up in this conversation. *I don't blame him*, Mandy thought. She felt awkward about it, too. *I hope India doesn't think her dad's visiting on Valentine's Day because he and Mrs. Arquette have changed their minds about being separated.* She tried to steer the conversation in a different direction. "I bet your dad will be glad to see Todd again."

"And I can't wait to see Dad," said India. "Todd and I miss him a lot. I know Mom does, too."

Darn. Mandy would have to think more carefully before she mentioned India's dad in the future. She wriggled her finger on the bed. Todd leaped off India's lap and pounced on Mandy's finger as if it was a mouse. She felt his little claws in her skin. They were incredibly sharp. "No wonder you managed to do so much damage," she said, easing her hand out of his grasp.

The kitten climbed up on her lap and rolled onto his back. He stretched himself out to his full length, then curled up snugly and purred, looking up at her with his beautiful amber eyes.

Mandy stroked his velvety brown coat. "You're totally adorable," she said as he folded his soft paws around her hand. "You know that no one could be angry with you for long!"

Three

"Has there been a big demand for deworming medication?" Mandy asked Jean the next morning. She was helping her sort through a delivery of veterinary supplies, including several boxes of worming tablets.

"You can say that again," said Jean. "Thanks to your poster, nearly everyone has asked for some."

"Great! A worm-free Welford," Mandy said. She took a box of sterile bandages to the storeroom. When she came back, she saw a tall figure walking up the drive. It was another frosty morning, and the man was dressed in a heavy overcoat. He was wearing a flat cap that gave away his identity at once. "Here comes Walter Pickard,"

Mandy said, craning her neck to see if he was carrying a cat carrier.

Walter Pickard was a retired butcher. He lived in one of the little houses behind the Fox and Goose, a few doors down from his good friend, Ernie Bell.

"I wonder what's up?" said Jean. She sat behind her desk and opened the blue appointment book. "He didn't make an appointment. And your mom and dad won't be able to see him yet."

Mandy's parents were in the surgery room, operating on a Rhodesian Ridgeback named Sultan. He had been hit by a car that morning and had a broken front leg.

"Not another crisis, I hope," Jean went on. "Does Walter have his cats with him?"

Walter's cats were named Tom and Flicker. Mandy felt especially close to Flicker. She'd rescued the black-and-white cat when floodwater had washed her down the river in a barrel, all the way to the front door of Animal Ark. Walter had adopted Flicker after his beloved cat, Scraps, had died.

"It doesn't look like it," said Mandy. "He isn't holding a carrier." She opened the door for Walter. "Is everything all right?"

"Yep. Tom and Flicker are great. They're curled up in front of the radiator as warm as toast." He stamped his feet on the doormat before coming inside. "It's all right

for some," he said with a smile and rubbed his hands
together to warm them up. He reached into the pocket
of his overcoat and pulled out a roll of paper. "I came
to ask if you would put this on your bulletin board."
He glanced at the board that was on the wall near
Jean's desk.

"What is it?" asked Jean.

"It's about a fund-raiser. For animals, of course," said
Walter. He unrolled the paper and held it up for Mandy
and Jean to read. At the top was a heading: WELFORD
WILDLIFERS. Walter was the secretary of the organization,
and an expert on wildlife in the area.

Mandy scanned the notice. It gave details of a fund-
raising run early in March. The route would be across
the fields up to the Beacon and back again, ending at
the village hall where a buffet lunch would be served.
"Are you entering?" she asked Walter.

"Me?" He laughed, pushing back his cap. "I'm too old
to run a race now. But I'll be one of the race officials."

"What's this about wild animal costumes?" Jean
asked, pointing to the bottom of the notice.

"The runners have to dress up like wild animals,"
Walter explained. "There'll be a special prize for the
best costume."

"That sounds like fun," Mandy said. She took a jar of
pins off Jean's desk and gave them to Walter. "We'll

move the other notices so that yours can be in the middle of the board," she said.

"I hope we can count on you and James entering," Walter said.

"Definitely," Mandy promised. "I wonder what animal I should be? A badger?"

Walter studied her for a moment. "You're too tall," he decided. "What about a deer?"

"That's more like it." Jean chuckled. "Especially with

those long legs of yours, Mandy. Of course, you could always be a giraffe."

"No good," said Walter, pinning up the notice. "It has to be a local animal." He looked at Mandy's poster which was on the opposite wall. "Now that's what I call a decent advertisement. And it's probably the closest I'll get to a Valentine," he joked. "Actually, Tom and Flicker are due for deworming. Thanks for the reminder, Mandy."

Just then the phone rang. Mandy answered it. "Animal Ark. May I help you?"

It was Lydia. "Good morning, Mandy. Can I speak to your mom or dad?"

"They're in the operating room right now. Can I give them a message?"

"It's Jemima," said Lydia. "She's scratching herself a lot, like she's got a skin irritation. I don't think it's serious but I'd like your mom or dad to have a look at her."

"I'll let them know as soon as they're out of surgery."

"Thanks, Mandy. But tell them not to go out of their way. Just to drop by next time they're passing by."

Ten minutes later, Dr. Adam Hope came through to the reception area. Walter had left, taking two deworming tablets with him, and Jean and Mandy were packing away the rest of the veterinary supplies in a cupboard behind the desk.

"How's Sultan?" Mandy asked.

"Groggy, but fine," said her dad, picking up the phone. "It wasn't a bad break so he'll be able to go home in a couple of days. I'm calling his owner now to say she can visit him this afternoon."

"That *is* good news," Mandy said. "But how will Sultan get around while his leg's healing?"

"Better than you can imagine," said her dad, dialing the number. "He'll learn to walk on three legs before you know it. Tracy?" he said as someone at the other end of the line answered the phone. "It's Adam Hope. Sultan's out of surgery and he's going to be fine. Feel free to come and see him in a couple of hours, once the anesthetic's worn off."

"By the way," Mandy said when her dad had finished talking to Sultan's owner, "Lydia thinks Jemima's got a skin problem. She'd like you to have a look at her when you have a chance."

"Actually, I was planning to take a drive up there after this morning's surgery," said Dr. Adam. He glanced around and lowered his voice. "I thought I'd surprise your mom with some goat's milk treats for Valentine's Day. It'll be a change from chocolates and flowers."

"What's that about flowers?" Dr. Emily came out from the consulting room.

Dr. Adam pretended to be puzzled. "Who said

anything about flowers? We were talking about, uh, about . . ."

"Showers," Mandy said quickly. She looked outside. The sun was shining out of a clear blue sky! "Dad hopes we won't have any showers."

Her mom looked at her skeptically. "And I hope that we will — showers of chocolates *and* flowers."

Lydia was surprised to see Mandy and her dad so soon. "You didn't have to go out of your way," she said when they arrived at the farm.

"We didn't," said Mandy. "Dad came to do his Valentine's shopping!"

"But we'll take a look at Jemima first," said Dr. Adam.

They waited while Lydia pulled on a pair of muddy rubber boots, then followed her across the yard to the barn.

"The herd is out in the fields," she explained. "It's such a lovely day, I thought they'd like to be out in the sunshine for a couple of hours. But Jemima's inside. Just until I know what's bothering her."

"How's Houdini today?" Mandy asked. "No windshield wiper side effects?"

"None at all. He's up to his usual tricks," said Lydia. "I caught him eating a plastic flower pot this morning."

Jemima's pen was at the far end of the barn. She

peered through the keyhole-shaped opening in the gate and bleated as Mandy, her dad, and Lydia approached her. *She must be lonely*, Mandy guessed. *And wondering why she can't be out in the fields with the others.*

"All right, Jemima. I'm here now," said Lydia. She opened the gate.

Mandy noticed that Ernie had painted it with the wood treatment so that it looked as good as new. *But that stuff smells horrible*, she thought, wrinkling her nose.

"What's troubling you, Jemima?" asked Dr. Adam, putting his vet's bag on the ground.

The dark gray goat scratched her shoulder with her hind leg. Mr. Hope looked closely at where she'd been scratching. "Nothing obvious. But it's a little dark in here. Let's take her outside."

They headed into the yard, Lydia leading Jemima by the collar. Dr. Adam examined the goat thoroughly, parting the fur where she'd been scratching. "Skin looks okay. No redness or rashes." He took her temperature. "That's normal," he said. "Is she eating well?"

Lydia shrugged. "I'm not sure. She was drooling and smacking her lips this morning, as if she'd eaten something she didn't like."

"She hasn't been munching on rhododendrons?" Mandy asked, remembering that the plant was deadly poisonous to goats. Once, Houdini had nearly died after escaping into Sam Western's garden and eating lots of the glossy green leaves.

Lydia shook her head. "You won't find a single rhododendron here."

Dr. Hope was trying to open Jemima's mouth but the goat kept pulling her head away. "Hold her for me please, Mandy."

Mandy put both hands firmly around Jemima's head. "Be a good girl for one second."

The goat was surprisingly strong. Mandy could feel her neck muscles pushing against her hands as she tried to pull away. But Mandy managed to keep her still long enough for her dad to check inside her mouth.

"Looks like she's got a small ulcer inside one cheek," he said. "That might explain the drooling." He let go of Jemima. She snapped her mouth shut and bleated angrily at him. "But it doesn't explain the itching."

"I've been rubbing that antihistamine cream, Itch-go, into her coat," said Lydia. "But it doesn't seem to be helping."

"Mmm," murmured Dr. Hope. Mandy could tell he was baffled. "Is she behaving normally?"

"As normally as goats can behave," said Lydia. "She was going around in circles in her pen early this morning and . . ."

"Circling?" Dr. Adam looked alarmed.

"But that's just because she was bored," said Lydia. "She stopped acting up when I took her out for some fresh air for five minutes."

Dr. Adam's expression relaxed. "OK."

Lydia let go of Jemima's collar. The goat nudged her hand then trotted over to a wooden fence and started nibbling at it.

"Silly goat. She'll end up with splinters," muttered Lydia. "It's just as well Ernie will be treating that fence when he's finished in the barn. She won't chew it then."

"Chewing on splintery wood is probably how she got the blister in her mouth," said Dr. Adam. He took a tube out of his bag and gave it to Lydia. "Try this antihistamine cream for the itching. It's stronger than Itch-go. If Jemima gets any worse, or any of the other goats start scratching, give me a call and I'll do some skin tests."

"I will," Lydia promised.

Mr. Hope closed his bag. "In the meantime, keep her in a stall alone, just in case it's something contagious." He opened the back of the Land Rover and put his bag inside. "Now, about that Valentine's shopping. What do you recommend for Emily?"

"I've got a few new products," said Lydia. "You can come have a look as soon as I've put Jemima away."

"I'll take her," Mandy offered.

"All right. You can put her in the pen just inside the door — it's far enough away from the others," said Lydia.

Jemima's new pen was badly in need of Ernie's care. The wooden gate and the panels on each side of the stall were rough and splintery, and looked as if they would fall down if someone gave them a good push. "Sorry it's a little run-down, Jemima, but I don't suppose you'd notice, anyway," Mandy said.

Jemima looked at her with dull eyes. There wasn't a trace of her normally sweet expression.

"Don't worry, girl," Mandy said, stroking her head, "You'll be feeling much better soon." She filled up the drinking pail with fresh water, and checked that there was enough fresh hay before heading into the farmhouse.

She found her dad and Lydia in the kitchen. Lydia's scrubbed pine dining table was a jumble of books and goat's milk products; there was hardly enough space on it for a plate or even a mug. Mandy wondered if Lydia ever sat down there to eat.

Dr. Adam looked bewildered as he pondered the homemade items in front of him. "I know Emily likes your soap. And the cream cheese in the heart-shaped molds looks great," he said. "So I'll take some of them.

I'm not sure about the pasta sauce, though. Not for Valentine's anyway."

"No. It's not exactly a romantic item," agreed Lydia. "Would she like these?" She picked up a plastic container and took off the lid. Inside were about ten beige-colored squares.

"What are they?" Mandy asked.

"Goat's milk fudge. My latest invention. Have a taste." She offered them to Mandy and her dad.

"Mmm, thanks," said Dr. Adam, helping himself to the biggest piece. "I love fudge."

Mandy took a more modest piece and popped it in her mouth. It was extremely sweet, but still had the distinctive strong flavor of goat's milk. Mandy wasn't sure it worked with fudge.

"What do you think?" Lydia prompted.

Mandy swallowed. "It's, um . . . interesting." She looked at her dad. His eyes were wide and his cheeks bulged as if he didn't like the flavor at all. *Serves him right for taking such a big piece!*

Suddenly, he swallowed. "Thanks, Lydia," he gulped. "It's solid, sweet fudge all right."

"You really think so?" Lydia looked relieved. "I know goat's milk isn't to everyone's taste so I used a lot of sugar to balance the flavor."

"It'll certainly appeal to people with a sweet tooth," said Dr. Adam. "No more for me right now, thanks, Lydia," he added as she offered him the container again. "I'm watching my waistline."

Lydia put the lid back on the box. "I hope it'll be popular. I've made several dozen boxes already."

Mandy wasn't sure that many people would like the fudge. But it would be awful if Lydia ended up being disappointed. "We'll be your first customers, won't we, Dad?" she said.

Her dad looked a bit shocked, then recovered quickly when Lydia looked delighted. "Yes, of course. We'll take a whole box!"

Four

"What did you expect me to say to Lydia?" Mandy asked her dad when they were driving home a short while later. He'd just accused her of scheming against him during the fudge episode. "That it tastes terrible, and I don't think anyone will want to buy it?"

"No. But you didn't have to pretend it was delicious," said Dr. Adam.

"I didn't. I just didn't want to hurt Lydia's feelings."

Her dad looked down at the plastic tub on the seat between him and Mandy. It was packed with goat's milk fudge. Lydia had insisted on giving Dr. Adam an extra pound for free. "In return for coming up to see Jemima so quickly. And also because you like fudge so much," she'd told him.

"Don't worry. We can always give it away," Mandy said as they continued down the overgrown farm road.

"To whom?" her father asked. "I bet even James won't eat it."

"Probably not," said Mandy. Like her dad, James loved food. But something he definitely didn't like was goat's milk.

They were driving past the Welford post office when Mandy saw India going inside. "Drop me off here, Dad. I'll walk home. I want to talk to India."

"You mean you want to find out how that kitten is?" Dr. Adam asked, smiling.

"That, too," Mandy said, jumping out of the Land Rover. She waved to her dad as he drove off, then went up the steps and pushed open the door.

A small bell rang, announcing her arrival. The post-lady, Mrs. McFarlane, was doing some paperwork at the counter. She greeted Mandy with a nod and went back to her work.

India was studying the greeting cards on display. She looked around as Mandy came over. "Hi, Mandy. Are you buying a card, too?"

Mandy hadn't planned to, but India's question gave her an idea. "Yes, I am, actually. For Walter Pickard."

"Who's he?"

Mandy told India about Walter, and his joke about the deworming-tablet poster being the nearest thing to a Valentine he'd get. "I'll send him an anonymous card," she decided, flicking through the cards on the stand. "This one's perfect!" On the front was a picture of a black-and-white kitten sitting on a red heart-shaped cushion. It had green eyes, and was wearing a red bow around its neck. "This is the spitting image of Walter's cat Flicker," Mandy said.

"It's cute," said India. "Almost as nice as Todd."

"How is he?"

"He's great," India smiled. "And he hasn't misbehaved or been too sick again."

"Oh, good. Maybe he just needed to settle down."

"Maybe," agreed India. "I can't wait for when I can let him out and he can explore his new home."

Mandy felt pleased to hear this. Not only did Todd seem to be adapting to his new environment but India was, too. She'd just referred to it as Todd's "new home." Did she think of it in the same way for herself?

Mandy watched India choose one of the biggest cards on display. The picture on the front was of two tabby kittens curled up in a basket. Inside, the greeting read, VALENTINE'S HUGS AND KISSES.

"Who's your Valentine?" Mandy teased.

"This isn't going to be from me," said India. "I'm sending it to Dad from Mom."

Mandy was shocked. "Oh," was all she could say.

India must have seen her surprise because she quickly said, "Mom's so busy unpacking and getting ready to start her new job, she doesn't have time to come out and choose a card."

"Did she *ask* you to come and buy one?" Mandy said. She couldn't imagine her mom sending her out to buy a Valentine's card. Not only that, but sending it for her too.

"Well . . . not really," said India. "But, like I told you, she's really stressed out. This is one way I can help her. And I know she'd like this card."

Mandy was bewildered. It seemed kind of personal to send a card for someone else — plus her mom had said Mr. and Mrs. Arquette were getting divorced. "Are you going to show it to your mom before you send it?"

India started to answer, but was stopped by the jangling bell. Mandy looked around as the door burst open and banged against the wall.

"Hey! Be careful," Mrs. McFarlane said to a man who was struggling to carry a huge cardboard box through the doorway. He bumped into a magazine stand, which wobbled wildly for a moment, shedding several newspapers. Mandy picked them up and put them back in the stand.

"Thank you, Amanda." Mrs. McFarlane came out from behind the counter, tut-tutting impatiently. "You can put the package there," she said, pointing to the floor in front of the man.

"Where?" the man mumbled from behind the box. It was so big, he couldn't see over the top, or even around the sides.

"On the floor in front of you," Mandy explained.

Awkwardly, the man lowered the bulky box to the ground. "Thanks," he puffed, standing up again. He took a delivery note out of his pocket and gave it to Mrs. McFarlane to sign. When he went back outside, he seemed to take extra care in closing the door behind him.

"Good. There's no need to bang doors," said Mrs. McFarlane. "Now let's see." She put her hands on her hips and looked at the parcel. "Where would be the best place for this, I wonder?"

"What's inside?" Mandy asked.

"Chocolates," answered the postmistress. She took a pair of scissors out of her overalls pocket and began cutting the string around the box. "Special ones for Valentine's Day." The string fell away and she opened the flaps on top of the box. "What do you think of this, girls?" She reached into the box and brought out a heart-shaped box that was covered in red satin.

"It's gorgeous!" exclaimed India.

"The contents are just as fabulous," said Mrs. McFarlane. "Luxury Belgian chocolate hearts."

"What about arranging them in a big heart in the window?" India suggested.

"That's a great idea," said Mrs. McFarlane. "We'll make a lovely red satin heart from the individual boxes."

There were fifty boxes of candy hearts in the parcel. Mandy and India helped Mrs. McFarlane unpack and arrange them in the window. While they were working, Ernie Bell stopped to peer through the glass. Mandy greeted him with a wave and a smile, and Mrs. McFarlane sang out, "Happy Valentine's Day, Ernie."

"It's a little early for that," he called and hurried away.

"I don't think all this romance is quite his style," Mandy said.

Mrs. McFarlane chuckled. "He probably thinks it's much too frivolous."

Even before the display was complete, people started coming in to buy the candy. One of the first was Mandy's grandfather, Tom Hope. "Not a word to Grandma," he warned Mandy as he put the box of candy in his shopping bag.

"Not even a hint, I promise," Mandy said, thrilled that her grandmother was in for such a lovely surprise.

Joanna Davey, who lived next to the post office, came in to buy some stamps. She left a few minutes later with a box of the chocolate hearts, too. They were for her husband, John.

"At this rate, all the boxes will be sold in no time," said Mrs. McFarlane after Joanna had closed the door behind her.

"A little like our deworming medication," Mandy said.

Mrs. McFarlane gave her an odd look. "Deworming medication?"

Mandy explained about the poster at Animal Ark and how it had caused a surge in sales.

Mrs. McFarlane laughed. "It just shows how many benefits there are to Valentine's Day." She picked up the last box of chocolate hearts and studied the display. "Now, where should we put this?" The big heart was complete, leaving no obvious place for the remaining chocolates.

"I'll buy it," said India, taking some money out of her purse.

Mandy felt nervous. What was India planning now?

"Are you sure, India?" asked Mrs. McFarlane. "Wouldn't you rather look for something less expensive?"

India shook her head. "They're exactly what I want, and if I don't buy them now, I might miss out." She gave Mrs. McFarlane the money. "Is that enough for the card, too?"

"It's more than enough. And because you helped me with the display, I'll give you a special price on the candy," said the postmistress. She gave the satin-covered box to India.

"Thanks! Dad loves Belgian chocolate," said India.

Oh no! Mandy's worst suspicions were confirmed.

Sending her dad a Valentine's card on behalf of her mom was bad enough, but to give him a heart-shaped box of candy was plain crazy. Mrs. Arquette might even be angry when she found out.

Mandy *had* to say something. "Are you sure you're doing the right thing? I mean, those chocolates are really expensive."

"It doesn't matter. They're perfect," India insisted.

"The thing is . . ." Mandy struggled to find the right words. "Maybe you shouldn't send the candy to your dad. He might —"

"I'm not sending it to him," India interrupted.

Mandy felt very relieved. "So you *do* have a Valentine!"

India shook her head. "No, the candies are for Mom and Dad to share when Dad visits us."

Uh-oh, thought Mandy. *She's determined to make Valentine's Day really special for her parents.* She didn't know what else to say. India was obviously hoping her parents would get back together again on the most romantic day of the year. Mandy just hoped she wouldn't be horribly disappointed.

Five

"Would you like to come to my house for lunch?" India asked as they were putting on their coats to leave the post office. "Mom won't mind. And Todd would love to see you again."

"I can't wait to see him, either," Mandy said. "I'd better call home first to tell my mom and dad where I'm going."

"The phone's over there," said Mrs. McFarlane, pointing to the counter.

Mandy dialed the Animal Ark number and her dad answered. "Don't be back too late, sweetie. We've got a busy afternoon and we might need your help."

As far back as she could remember, Mandy had helped her mom and dad in the clinic. When she was younger, she'd had simple duties like sweeping out the residential unit where sick animals, or those recovering from operations, were kept. But over the years, she'd taken on more challenging tasks like changing the dressings on animals after they'd had surgery.

"I'll be home right after lunch," Mandy promised her dad. She loved every minute she spent helping animals.

Mrs. Arquette was painting the living-room ceiling when Mandy and India arrived. They didn't go in to see her, because India wanted to hide the box of candy hearts first. But Mandy caught a glimpse of Mrs. Arquette through the door. She was standing on a ladder, a brush in one hand. Mrs. Arquette's sweater and jeans were splattered with paint, and she had a scarf around her head.

"I brought Mandy home for lunch," India called out. "But we'll go up and see Todd first."

"Great!" Mrs. Arquette called back. "There's a pizza in the oven."

Just like before, India opened her bedroom door carefully to make sure Todd didn't slip out. But this time his little face didn't appear in the gap.

"I hope he hasn't escaped," India said, sounding worried. She opened the door wider.

A bump under the bedspread caught Mandy's eye. It moved just slightly, but enough for Mandy to know what it was. "It's all right. He's just playing hide-and-seek in your bed!"

"Phew!" India sighed. She put the box of candy on her bedside table and peeled back the bedspread. Todd was curled up in the middle of the bed with his nose tucked under his tail.

"You scared me," said India, scooping him up and kissing the top of his head. "I thought you snuck out."

Todd snuggled up against her, purring loudly enough for Mandy to hear him. "He's really happy to see you," she said. She sat down and put her hand out to pet him, but he grabbed it in his paws and held on tightly.

"Careful what you do with those little fish hooks of yours," Mandy warned with a smile. She unhooked his claws one by one but as soon as she freed her hand, Todd pounced and grabbed Mandy's hand again.

"Todd!" said India.

"He's only playing." Mandy rolled her hand into a fist to protect her fingers from the kitten's lightning-fast reactions. "It's all part of practicing to be a big hunter someday. He's just like his cousins really, lions and leopards and all the other big cats. "

"I guess so," said India.

"Except that he's a lot tamer," Mandy said. Todd was licking her fingers. His tongue felt like sandpaper! "That's better than feeling your claws in me," she said, scratching him behind his ear.

Something must have distracted him because he jumped off the bed and scampered across the floor. As Mandy watched him, she noticed a red T-shirt on the floor beneath India's desk. There was a hole in one sleeve, and shreds of the red fabric on the carpet around it. "Uh-oh, I think Todd's been up to his tricks again."

"Don't say that," groaned India. She bent down to pick up the ruined T-shirt. "It's my favorite, too." She frowned at the kitten who was sitting on the carpet nearby. He stared up at her. "You're very bad!" said India. She picked him up and put him back on the bed.

Todd bounded across the bed, clambered up to the pillow, and leaped onto the bedside table — right on top of the box of candies.

"Hey! Get off there," said India, grabbing him before he could do any more damage. She put him back on the bed next to Mandy and sat down on the other side of him.

He rolled over and looked at her upside down, as if he couldn't imagine what all the fuss was about.

"And now you're pretending to be innocent," said

India. "You're going to have to learn a few manners, you know."

"He is misbehaving," Mandy agreed. "But it's hard to train cats. They're such independent animals." She scratched his chest. "You only thought you were playing, didn't you, Todd?"

The kitten seemed to love being the center of attention. He purred like a smoothly running engine, and Mandy felt his throat and chest vibrating softly. "I bet he gets a little bored when you're not around," she said to India.

"But I can't be with him all the time."

"I know," Mandy said sympathetically. "And it's even trickier right now because he has to be shut in while he gets used to his new environment."

"I do take him downstairs sometimes," said India. Todd rolled onto his tummy, and India ran her hand along his back and down his thick tail. "But we have to be careful because Mom's painting some of the rooms. She'd be furious if there were chocolate-colored hairs stuck everywhere."

"That wouldn't be good," Mandy agreed. She chuckled as Todd climbed onto her lap, stood up on his back legs and started biting one of the buttons on her shirt.

Mrs. Arquette called up to them, "The pizza is ready, girls!"

"Coming, Mom!" called India. "Can Todd come down, too?"

"As long as he behaves himself and stays in the kitchen," said Mrs. Arquctte.

During lunch, Todd explored every nook and cranny in the kitchen. He poked his front paws into the gaps between cupboards, inspected a basket of clean laundry, and checked to see what was behind the ironing board leaning against the wall.

"You know what curiosity did?" Mandy said as she watched him slide his paws beneath the fridge.

"What?" asked India.

"It killed the cat," said her mom.

India looked appalled. "That's terrible!"

"It's just a saying," her mom reassured her.

"And we're keeping a close eye on him so he won't get hurt," Mandy said, watching Todd do his best to squeeze behind the fridge.

"So don't let him do that, India," said Mrs. Arquette. "If he gets behind there, he might not be able to get out again."

India grabbed Todd before he could disappear behind the fridge. "No, you don't!" She sat down with him on her lap, but he was like a grasshopper. He sprang onto the floor, and scooted over to his own lunch — a little portion of fish served in his paw-patterned dish. He took a mouthful and before he'd even swallowed it, he was off again, bounding over to a paint can standing on a sheet of newspaper on the floor in the corner.

"Oops!" Mandy exclaimed as he jumped effortlessly on top of it. Luckily, the lid was on. Mandy relaxed. "I thought he was about to turn into a white Burmese."

Todd crouched on top of the can with his front legs dangling over the edge. He dabbed at the drips on the sides and waved his tail from side to side.

"I wish I had a camera," said India. "He looks so sweet."

"You'd have to be quick," her mom said as Todd jumped down again.

Landing on the newspaper, he started shredding it with his claws. There was a mischievous glint in his eyes. He looked impish and a little wild like his bigger relatives, Mandy decided.

In no time at all, the kitten had ripped the paper to pieces. *He's like a miniature paper-shredding machine*, Mandy thought. Then she saw there were a lot of white paw prints on the floor. His feet must have soaked up the drips on the side of the tin.

Mrs. Arquette was not amused. "That's enough. I have to do enough cleaning up already without having to wipe up after a cat. If he can't behave himself, he'll have to go upstairs."

India gulped down the last of her pizza. "We're done, anyway," she said, scooping him up.

Back upstairs, India made sure Todd's paws were clean before she put him on her bed. He curled up next to a teddy bear and fell asleep.

"I'm not surprised he's exhausted after the way he ran around during lunch," Mandy said, sitting next to him. She noticed that the teddy bear looked moth-eaten in a few places. "More Todd treatment?" she asked, pointing to a hole in the toy's ear.

"Yes, he loves chewing it. But I don't mind. I got the teddy bear in France when Dad and I were on vacation there just before I got Todd. He liked it the first day he was with me."

"Maybe it reminded him of his littermates because it's furry and warm," Mandy said. "At least it turned out to be a useful souvenir."

"Actually, it was a prize in a skiing competition."

"Really?" Mandy was impressed. "I love skiing, but I don't think I'm good enough to win a prize." She watched Todd uncurl himself and roll over. He stretched his legs then, like an elastic band springing back to size, he curled up tightly again.

"It was just a beginner's competition," said India. She went over to a small bookshelf beneath the window and took an album off the bottom shelf. "Do you want to see the photos?"

"I'd love to."

They sat together on the edge of the bed and went through the pictures. Most of them were of India, looking very sporty in her blue-and-white ski suit. The photographs showed her going up a slope in the ski lift, or learning how to do snow plows, or practicing on the bunny slopes. A few were of her lying sprawled out on the ground, laughing.

"I got very used to falling down," she joked. "And I wasn't the only one." She turned to the next page. One of the pictures was of a man flat on his back on a slope, his skis standing up at awkward angles. He was laughing up at the camera, his blue eyes squinting against the bright sun. "Even Dad fell over a few times."

"At least he seemed to find it funny," Mandy said. "He must have a good sense of humor."

"He does," said India. "He's really fun to be with."

A rustling noise made Mandy turn round. Todd had woken up and was inspecting the chocolate hearts again, sniffing eagerly at the box, and prodding it with one paw. "Not again . . ." Mandy began but before she could get up, Todd had managed to nudge the lid off with his nose. In less than a heartbeat, he sprang into the middle, landing with all four paws in the chocolates.

"Todd!" cried India, jumping up. "Get out of there."

"I think it's too late," Mandy said as the kitten sat down on top of the candies. With the shiny red fabric crumpled up around him, he looked as if he had just popped out of a present. Mandy leaned across and lifted Todd out of the box.

India stared down at the candies. "He's ruined them!" She snapped the album shut and put it down hard on the bed.

"That's really bad luck," Mandy said. She was very concerned because it looked like Todd had taken a mouthful of candy when he jumped into the box. There were smears of chocolate on his whiskers and around his mouth, and chocolaty smudges on his already chocolate-colored paws. "Don't say you've eaten some of them, you silly boy," she said.

"He's not silly," said India. "He's incredibly bad. And now he's spoiled my Valentine's surprise."

"You're going to have to keep an eye on him," Mandy warned, wiping the sticky smudges off the kitten's cheeks and paws with a tissue. "Chocolate can be dangerous for some cats."

India looked anxiously at Mandy. "What do you mean?"

"There's a chemical called theobromine in chocolate that can be poisonous for a lot of dogs and for some cats."

India gasped. "Does that mean he's been poisoned?"

"No, because not every cat who eats chocolate will get sick, and it's mainly dogs who are affected," said Mandy. "Plus, I don't think Todd ate very much." She picked up the candy-heart box and studied the chocolates. Except for one or two that looked a bit squashed, they were all still whole. There was also an equal number of chocolates and the paper casings that held them. "None missing," she said. "Todd must have just had a taste." She wiped off a smudge on his cheek with a clean tissue. As she did, the kitten opened his mouth and Mandy saw that his gums were bright red. "Gosh!"

"Now what?"

"I'm not sure," Mandy said. "It might not be important, but . . ." She really didn't want to worry India any more.

"But what?"

"It's just that his gums look a little on the red side." Mandy gently pushed back Todd's lip for another look. He shook his head and pushed away her finger with his paw. Was it because his mouth hurt?

"Is it bad to have red gums?" asked India.

"Well, it could mean that they are sore." Mandy

thought hard. Sore red gums meant inflammation, which could be caused by an infection or a disease. "Gingivitis, maybe?" she said out loud, recalling a term she'd heard her parents use.

"What's that?" said India, going pale.

"It's a disease when the gums get infected. It can lead to a lot of other problems, I think," Mandy said. She seemed to remember that if it wasn't treated, it could cause kidney problems.

"You're saying that on top of everything, he's really sick after all?" asked India.

Mandy shook her head. "No. Only that he could become ill if it *is* gingivitis."

India shook her head. "I never thought owning a kitten would be so difficult."

"I guess you can't tell before you get an animal just how much responsibility it'll mean," Mandy said, petting Todd. She was starting to wish she hadn't said anything to India. It might have been better if she'd told her mom and dad about Todd's red gums first. "Look, if it is gingivitis," she said, "it must be in the early stages, otherwise Mom would have noticed when she examined Todd the other day."

"Yes, but it'll still mean he's got a disease," said India, looking very unhappy.

"I know. But there are things you can do. Like clean

his teeth, and make sure he keeps away from food he shouldn't have." She tapped the kitten's mouth gently. "Like chocolate."

Todd batted her finger. Mandy curled her hand up before he could sink his claws into it again.

"I wish I'd known about all this before now," India said miserably.

"Don't worry," Mandy said. "That's what vets are for, to help you learn about caring for your pet."

"Mom and Dad should have known," India went on. "But Mom's too busy with everything, and Dad . . . well, if he was here, he'd have figured things out for me." Her voice trembled, and Mandy realized she was on the verge of tears.

"It'll be okay, India," she promised. "We've just got to keep a closer eye on this little guy." She lifted Todd up and held him in front of her. "I tell you what. I'll bring him a special toothbrush for cats, and animal tooth-paste next time I come over. And we'll get my mom to check out his mouth."

"Thanks," said India. "We're really lucky we met you!"

Todd was struggling in Mandy's hands. She put him on the bed and he scampered straight back to the candy-heart box. Mandy grabbed him before he could sink his teeth into the chocolates again. "Enough is enough," she said.

India sighed. "He'll never learn."

"Don't worry," Mandy said. "I bet as soon as he's allowed outdoors to explore and hunt, he won't be half as mischievous."

But India didn't look at all convinced. In fact, the gloomy expression on her face suggested that she was starting to get fed up with Todd for all the trouble he was causing.

Six

"I think Todd's got gingivitis," Mandy announced to her parents during breakfast the next morning. They'd been very busy when Mandy returned home the day before, and in the evening they'd gone to a meeting so there hadn't been time to tell them about the kitten's latest escapade.

"What makes you think that?" asked her mom, looking up from the morning paper.

Mandy put two slices of bread in the toaster. "His gums are very red and swollen."

"That doesn't automatically mean gingivitis," said her dad, pouring himself a cup of tea.

Dr. Emily closed the paper. "Todd's too young to have gingivitis. And anyway, I'd have noticed it when I examined him the other day. Red gums could simply mean that he's teething."

This hadn't even crossed Mandy's mind. She snapped her fingers. "Of course! He's exactly the right age to be growing new teeth." The toast popped out. It was piping hot and burned her fingers. "Ouch!" She dropped it onto the counter and went to get a plate from the table. "I suppose that could be why he keeps chewing things."

"Could be," said Dr. Emily.

"Which means I scared India for nothing," Mandy said glumly, sitting down again. "When I left her yesterday, she was really worried about Todd. And that's on top of being upset over her parents."

"Divorce is very difficult for everyone involved," said Dr. Emily. "And unfortunately, there isn't much we can do to make things better for India through this tough time. Except of course to be her friend, and help her with Todd."

"That I definitely can do," Mandy said.

Dr. Adam stretched across the table for the newspaper. "You could show her how to keep his teeth clean, especially if he's a chocolate nibbler. That's one way of preventing gingivitis."

Mandy smiled. "I've already promised to take her a toothbrush and some toothpaste for him."

"One step ahead of your dad, again! Sometimes I think I could let you take over my job."

When she'd finished her breakfast, she went to the storeroom to choose a toothbrush for Todd. She'd just settled on a little blue one when she heard the phone ring in the reception area. Jean hadn't arrived yet, So Mandy went to answer it. But her dad was already there. He was standing at Jean's desk with the receiver to his ear.

"Are you sure it's the same?" Mandy heard him ask. "No other symptoms that you've noticed?" He listened for a second, then said, "I'll come up right away." He hung up, looking solemn.

"What is it?" Mandy asked.

"That was Lydia. Jemima's much better."

"Great. But then why do you have to rush up to High Cross Farm?" Mandy asked.

"There's bad news, too," said Dr. Adam.

Mandy felt her stomach twist in a knot.

"Three more goats are showing the same symptoms."

"You mean itchy skin?" Mandy said.

"Yes. And salivation. A little motor confusion, too . . .

walking in circles, that kind of thing." He went through to his consulting room and opened his vet's bag.

Mandy followed him in and watched him check the contents. "What do you think it means?"

"I'm not sure." Dr. Adam put a small silver flashlight in the bag. "It could be nothing, like it seems to have been with Jemima. Or it could be more serious."

Mandy felt the knot in her stomach tighten. "What sort of serious illness?"

"Let's not jump to conclusions," said her dad. "Let's first find out exactly what's going on at High Cross Farm."

Mandy knew the moment she saw the three goats that they were much worse off than Jemima had been. Even from a distance, they looked thoroughly miserable and they were scratching themselves constantly. *It's like they're crawling with lice*, Mandy thought.

Lydia had put them in a section of the yard that Ernie had fenced off recently, where Mandy's dad would be able to have a good look at them. It was a cold, overcast day, the low, gray clouds threatening to burst at any moment. Just the sort of weather to make a grim situation seem even worse.

The sick goats were huddled together in one corner. As she went closer, Mandy recognized the three. There was Lady Jayne, a brown nanny goat with a white face and big brown eyes fringed with long lashes. One of Lydia's favorites was there, too, a young ram named Monty. He was dark-faced and had a straggly beard and pitch-black coat. A nanny goat named Alexandra was the third one in the pen. Her light brown coat was normally shiny and soft-looking, but today it looked dry and dull.

"They must be feeling bad," Mandy said, leaning over the fence. She clapped her hands. "Come and see what I've got for you." She'd put a few slices of apple in her pocket at home, thinking the goats would enjoy them.

But the goats didn't even come over to sniff the treat. Instead, Lady Jane wandered over to a freshly treated fence post and rubbed her head against it. She rubbed and rubbed until Mandy started to worry she'd scrape her skin off. "We've got to stop her," she said to her dad.

Just then, Lydia hurried over from the barn. "Thank goodness you could come," she said. Her face was pinched, as if she couldn't bear seeing her goats in such distress. "What could it be, Adam?"

"I can't say for sure," said Dr. Adam. "I'll have to do some tests. First though, I'd like to see Jemima."

"She's still in the isolation pen," said Lydia.

Inside the barn, the rest of the herd peered out from their pens. Mandy felt a pang of sadness when she

noticed the empty stalls that normally housed the three goats outside. And when she looked at Houdini's enclosure, she saw he wasn't there, either. "Where's Houdini?"

"I had to put him outside so that Ernie can work on his pen," said Lydia. "He wanted to do it yesterday, but Houdini kept getting in the way and was trying to eat the paintbrushes."

Mandy had to smile as she pictured the mischievous goat thwarting Ernie in his work.

Jemima let them know how happy she was to see them by bleating and rubbing her head against Mandy's hand. Her eyes were bright and she wore her usual impish expression. This made Mandy feel a lot more positive about the three outside. If Jemima had recovered this quickly, they might, too.

"She looks in good shape to me," said Dr. Adam. "Let's just see if that mouth ulcer is gone." He took the flashlight out of his bag while Lydia led the goat from her stall.

Mandy held Jemima's head still while her dad pried the goat's mouth open to look inside.

"That's cleared up," said Dr. Adam, switching off the flashlight. "The itching must have been a minor skin irritation that responded to the new ointment." He snapped his bag shut. "Now let's see the other three."

Out in the yard, Alexandra was rubbing her sides along the fence. She was smacking her lips together, drooling. On the other side of the pen, Monty was trotting back and forth, restlessly kicking up his heels. Lady Jayne was still standing in front of the fence post, her head rammed against it as if she was trying to push it over.

Dr. Adam gave a low whistle. This bothered Mandy a lot. It usually meant her dad knew what he was facing, and that it was very, very serious.

"Lydia," said Dr. Adam. "I'm going to be frank about this."

Lydia's face went pale. "It's not good, is it?"

Mr. Hope shook his head. "No. The circling, the salivation, the generally odd behavior . . . I know I haven't examined the goats yet, but all those symptoms point to two possibilities."

Mandy held her breath.

"Scrapie. Or foot-and-mouth disease."

Mandy felt her heart skip a few beats. She knew how serious and how infectious both diseases were. Outbreaks of foot-and-mouth disease on farms often led to thousands of sheep and cattle being put down. There was no cure for the debilitating illness that left the animal with crippling ulcers on their hooves and inside their mouths. It was so contagious that the only way to stop it spreading to other farms was to destroy the whole herd.

And as for scrapie, she knew that it was mainly sheep that caught the disease and that there was no treatment for it, either. Was it as bad for goats?

Lydia stared at Mr. Hope. "Scrapie. Foot-and-mouth," she echoed. Her voice was hoarse. "I can't believe it. Not my goats. I do everything right with them."

Dr. Adam put his hand on Lydia's arm. "I know that. And I hope I'm wrong. I really do."

"You don't think they're just cold, or acting up because it's starting to rain?" Mandy said, clutching at straws. Lydia had once told her that the goats hated damp, that they panicked in the rain, and detested cold.

"No. This goes beyond normal anxiety," said Dr. Adam.

"But Jemima got better," Mandy pointed out. "And she was just the same as them."

"I thought so, too, for a while," said her dad. "But I'm not sure that it was the same thing after all." He went to the Land Rover where he put on a white coat and a pair of rubber boots. He slipped some plastic covers over the boots and pulled on a pair of latex gloves.

"What happens next?" Lydia asked.

"Let's see if we can rule out foot-and-mouth first. I'll examine them for that, and take some blood tests."

"And scrapie?" Mandy asked.

Her dad gave her an odd look. Without answering her, he went to open the gate to go into the pen.

"Dad?" Mandy prompted, following him. "Are you going to test for scrapie, too?"

Dr. Adam closed the gate behind him and turned round slowly. "I can't test for scrapie. Not unless . . ."

Mandy felt Lydia come up behind her and put a hand on her shoulder. "Not unless he puts the goats down first." Her voice was as flat as a still pond, but a tremor beneath it threatened to break the surface.

It was one of the worst moments of Mandy's life. Put the goats down! That was unthinkable. And what if it turned out not to be scrapie? "There has to be another way," she insisted.

Dr. Adam shook his head. "There isn't. Scrapie is a viral disease that affects the central nervous system. Basically, it makes holes in the brain so that it ends up looking like a sponge. The only way to make a definite diagnosis is to take a brain sample."

Mandy could hardly believe what she was hearing. Tears pricked her eyes as she watched her dad make his way over to Lydia's goats. Her precious and danger-ously ill goats.

A movement in the paddock that backed onto the barn caught Mandy's eye. Houdini was standing on a tall haystack next to the barn wall. Either he was trying to get a good view from there, or he intended to find a way out.

Typical Houdini, Mandy thought. He was full of personality and always up to something. *But for how much longer?* He looked great now, as fit as a fiddle. But was it too late to stop the infection — whatever it turned out to be — from spreading to him and the others? What would Lydia do if her entire herd had to be destroyed?

Seven

For once, Mandy couldn't help her dad examine the goats. "We didn't bring any protective clothing for you," he explained. "If it *is* foot-and-mouth, we can't risk spreading it. And if there's a chance it's scrapie, well . . ." He didn't finish, but Mandy understood how dangerous the situation was.

She and Lydia watched from outside the pen while Dr. Adam examined the goats' feet, and looked in their mouths and nostrils. He took some blood from each of them and checked their temperatures. "Normal temperatures, and no signs of blistering under the feet or in their nostrils," he announced when he'd finished. "Which means they don't have the typical symptoms of foot-and-mouth."

Mandy and Lydia exchanged a hopeful look.

"But I still can't rule it out," Dr. Adam continued. "And I'm a bit suspicious about some blisters in Monty's mouth. So until we know exactly what we're dealing with, these three will have to go into quarantine."

"We can use the old barn," said Lydia. "Will you help me get it ready, Mandy?"

They hurried around the farmhouse to a small, rather dilapidated barn.

"I never thought I'd have to use this again," Lydia said as they went in. "Otherwise I'd have asked Ernie to fix it up, too."

It was dark and musty-smelling inside. Mandy pushed the door wide open to let some air in before helping Lydia to drag in some bales of straw. They spread the straw on the ground, and brought in fresh hay. Mandy got some water in a pail and put it next to the hay. "I think we've made it as comfortable as we can," she said, taking a last look around before they went outside.

When Dr. Adam saw them returning, he brought Lady Jayne and Monty to the fence, holding them by their collars. Mandy opened the gate to let him out and he led the two away. On either side of him, the goats flicked their ears as if they were still feeling uncomfortable.

Dr. Adam came back after a few minutes and got Alexandra. Passing Mandy, the goat gave her a mournful look.

"Poor Alexandra," Mandy said, longing to stroke her. She wanted to tell her what she always told sick animals, that they'd soon be feeling better thanks to her parents' expert care. But she would be lying if she promised that now. Not even her dad, with all his experience, knew exactly what they were dealing with.

With the goats quarantined in the old barn, and the blood samples ready to be sent for analysis, there was nothing more to be done. Dr. Adam peeled off the latex gloves and the protective covering from his boots. "Get me a couple of trash bags from the Land Rover, please, Mandy," he said.

She brought them over and opened one of them.

Dr. Adam put the used items inside to be disposed of correctly later on. He took off his white coat and put that in the other bag. It would be thoroughly disinfected back at Animal Ark. "You'd better take your shoes off and put them in too, Mandy," he said. "We can't risk contaminating the Land Rover."

Mandy eased herself into the passenger seat, being careful not to let her shoes touch any part of the vehicle. She dropped them into the trash bag, then, making sure that her feet didn't touch the ground, she swung her legs inside.

Dr. Adam put the bags in the back of the Land Rover. "I'll let you know as soon as I get the results," he promised Lydia.

Lydia just nodded. "I can't believe it," she said over and over again.

As Mandy and her dad drove away from High Cross Farm, she looked back. Lydia was standing outside the empty pen. Drizzle swirled around Lydia, enveloping her like wet mist. Before Mandy and her dad had reached the end of the driveway, Lydia was no longer visible. It was as if the rain had swallowed her up.

"The goats looked so miserable!" Mandy was describing what had happened at High Cross Farm to James the next morning. They met outside the Fox and Goose on their way to see India and Todd. Mandy had called James the night before and briefly told him about the goats, promising to fill in all the details when she saw him.

They set off for the Arquettes' house. Normally, they'd have taken their bikes, but it was a frosty morning and the road was as slippery as glass, so they were on foot.

Mandy had the special toothbrush and paste for Todd in her pocket. She wanted to put India's mind at ease about the gingivitis, and to start Todd off on his teeth-cleaning routine. After getting back from High Cross Farm the day before and changing her clothes, she'd cycled over to the Arquettes' house. But since there was no one home, Mandy and James had decided to try again this morning.

As they walked along the sidewalk, the frost crunching beneath their boots, Mandy tried to imagine what Lydia was feeling right now. The foot-and-mouth results were due in a couple of days — just before Valentine's Day. What sort of day would it turn out to be for Lydia?

James must have been having similar thoughts. "Lydia's got to be horribly worried," he said.

"You can say that again," Mandy said. "You know how serious foot-and-mouth is."

"So that's definitely it?"

"Well, Dad hasn't ruled it out," said Mandy. "But he's more concerned it could be scrapie."

"Why?"

"The itching and the way the goats are behaving — sort of going around in circles," said Mandy. "Dad says that could be a lack of coordination, and that's one of the symptoms of scrapie."

They turned onto Playground Lane, the street where India and her mom lived. Mandy felt drained from all the anxiety over the goats, so she was looking forward to some fun with Todd. She had her fingers crossed that Todd hadn't gotten into any more mischief since the disaster with the candy hearts two days ago.

But when they reached the Arquettes' front door, it sounded like Todd had done something awful.

"That kitten has been nothing but trouble!" came Mrs. Arquette's voice from inside the house.

"He *hasn't*!" India shot back.

"Well, if you can't look after him properly . . ." her mom began, but India cut in, "I *can*," and Mandy glimpsed her hurrying past the hall window.

She must have spotted Mandy and James on the front porch because the door swung open. "The most terrible thing has happened!" she burst out.

"What?" Mandy and James asked in unison.

"Todd's vanished."

"No!" Mandy gasped.

"Do you mean hiding vanished, or lost vanished?" said James. "Or has he escaped?"

"I don't know," India moaned, and Mandy saw that she was fighting back tears.

"Because if he's hiding," James went on in his

practical voice, "then we'd better close the door in case he shoots out." He led Mandy and India into the hall and shut the door behind them. "And if he's lost or has escaped, then we'd better start looking for him right away."

"I *have* been looking for him," said India, sitting on the bottom stair. She put her elbows on her knees and cupped her chin in her hands. *"Everywhere."*

"I warned you something like this might happen," said

Mrs. Arquette, coming into the hall. She was wearing her paint-splattered clothes again, and her hair was bunched up under a scarf. "If you hadn't left your door open . . ."

"I *told* you. It was only for a few seconds while I went to the bathroom," said India.

Mrs. Arquette sighed. "A few seconds is all it takes."

Mandy hated being caught up in a private argument. She didn't know what to say.

"I'm sorry you've walked into a crisis," said Mrs. Arquette, as if she sensed Mandy was feeling uncomfortable.

"It's OK," Mandy said. "We can help look for him."

"Thanks," said Mrs. Arquette. "I've got so much to do. I don't have time to go chasing after a kitten."

James was already scouting around the hall. "He can't be far," he said, looking behind a big packing box. Not finding Todd there, he turned to the others. "Let's do this systematically. Mandy, you and India search upstairs. Take a different room each. I'll hunt down here."

"I've already searched everywhere," India reminded him.

"But he could be moving around, in which case you might have missed him," said her mom. "He could have even snuck into one of the boxes." She gestured toward the living room.

Mandy looked through the door and saw a half dozen big packing boxes in there. Most of them appeared to be half unpacked. Books and knickknacks were scattered around on the floor and stacked on the windowsills.

"I'll go through some more boxes now," said Mrs. Arquette. "Maybe I'll find him."

Mandy started in the bathroom. It took less than a minute for her to see that he wasn't in there. She crossed the landing and went into India's room. She searched under the bed, behind the curtains, even among the books on the bookshelf. *Not even a whisker.*

She went back onto the landing where she met India coming out of her mom's bedroom. "He's not in there," said India.

They headed down to the living room, pausing to check in the closet under the stairs. Nothing.

"Take a look around, but I'm sure he's not in here," said Mrs. Arquette when they joined her. She put a glass vase on the coffee table alongside some china ornaments, then reached into the packing box again. At her feet was a pile of crumpled-up newspaper that had been wrapped around the breakable items. If Todd had been there, he'd have probably made a beeline for it, Mandy thought with a pang. Shredding paper was one of his favorite games.

Todd wasn't in the living room or the dining room or the sunroom. "I've turned those rooms upside down," said James when they met up in the hall.

"That leaves the kitchen," Mandy said.

"He won't be there," said India. "Mom was painting in there before you came. She'd have definitely noticed him."

"It's the only place we haven't looked," argued James. "He must be in there."

But as soon as they went through the door, Mandy knew James was wrong. Todd wasn't in the kitchen. "The window's open," she said, pointing. "I think Todd got out."

Eight

Mandy rushed over to the window to take a closer look.

The window was above the sink, and the bottom pane was raised a few inches. The gap was just big enough for a slender Burmese kitten to slip through. And there was a trail of muddy pawprints leading from a potted plant next to the sink onto the ledge outside the window.

India leaned across the sink to look outside. "He could be anywhere!"

"He couldn't have gone very far," Mandy said. She craned her neck, hoping to see the kitten scampering across the lawn. All she saw was a big and neglected yard with lots of bushy shrubs and a sparse hedge at the back. On the other side of the street were the school's sports fields. Todd *could* be anywhere, and heading farther into the big wide world with every second.

Mrs. Arquette came into the kitchen. "Any luck yet?"

"He escaped!" India exclaimed. She pointed at the window. "It's *your* fault, Mom. You left the window open."

"Yes, I did. To let in some air after I'd finished painting the ceiling."

"And you let Todd out," said India.

"And you left your bedroom door open."

Mandy didn't think this would get them anywhere. She exchanged a glance with James and they headed quietly for the front door to start searching for Todd outside. But they could still hear India arguing with her mom. "You blame me for everything. Dad wouldn't be like that. He'd be on my side now."

The kitchen door slammed, and India stormed outside to join them. Her face was flushed. "If he ran away . . ." she began.

"He didn't," Mandy said, looking behind a holly bush. "He just came out to explore."

"Do you really think so?" said India, parting the prickly leaves and peering into the shrub.

Nearby, James was on his hands and knees,

searching among the frost-blackened remains of some cabbage plants. A blackbird hopped behind him, probably hoping that James would disturb some tasty earthworms.

When James stood up though, the bird flew up into an apple tree that was covered in early white blossoms, like delicate clusters of snow. Mandy saw it land on a branch. As soon as it settled, it gave a loud squawk and took off again.

Mandy squinted up at the tree to see what had startled the bird. A clump of blossom shifted, revealing a pointed chocolate-colored face.

"Todd!" Mandy cried.

"You found him!" India gasped, racing over to join her under the tree.

The kitten peeped out at them from behind the blossom. He edged forward, gripping the branch with his claws. *Meow!* he wailed.

"Come down, Todd," India urged, standing directly below the branch where he was crouching. She held out her arms as if she expected him to jump into them.

Mrs. Arquette was watching from the kitchen window. "Is he up there?" she called.

"Yes!" replied India.

Her mom came out at once. "Thank goodness you found him." She put her arm around India's shoulders and peered up at Todd. "Silly little cat, getting himself stuck up there."

Todd clung to his branch, his golden eyes wide and staring.

"I think he's too scared to move," Mandy said.

"I'll go up for him," said James, and started to climb the tree. But his sneakers slipped down the trunk every time he tried to boost himself up. He jumped up to grab the branch above him, but it was just out of reach. "It might be easier without shoes," he puffed. He kicked off his sneakers and pulled off his socks.

He was trying again when a familiar voice called out from the road. "What's going on?"

Mandy looked around to see Ernie peering over the fence, his van parked in the road behind him. "Is there a problem?"

"Yes. A kitten's stuck in the tree," Mandy called back.

"We can use my ladder," said Ernie. He quickly untied it from the roof of his van, then carried it into the yard. He propped the ladder against the trunk of the apple tree but it wasn't high enough to reach all the way up to Todd's branch.

"I'll just have to stretch when I get to the top," said Ernie, "and hope the kitten doesn't climb any higher."

James already had his foot on the bottom rung. "I'll get him. He might scratch you."

"I know all about kittens' claws," said Ernie. "Tiddles taught me about them long ago. But you go ahead. I'll hold the ladder."

Still barefoot, James swiftly climbed the ladder. At the top, he caught hold of a branch and climbed onto it. He stood up gingerly, grabbed another branch that was just in front of him, and reached up for the kitten.

Todd meowed and backed away.

"It's all right, Todd!" called India.

James stood on tiptoe to reach up higher. Mandy bit her lip. The branch he was standing on didn't look all that sturdy. It swayed and cracked loudly. Suddenly, to her horror, the end snapped off and fell to the ground.

She gasped as she saw James teeter, one foot slipping off the broken end. "Careful!" she cried.

But James was already steadying himself. He grabbed the branch in front of him with both hands and shuffled along the one he was standing on, away from the broken end.

Above him, and well out of reach, Todd stared at him in alarm, his eyes still like saucers.

Mrs. Arquette looked worried. "Come down, James. The tree's not strong enough to hold you."

"I'm okay," said James. He reached up again. "Here, Todd."

Todd's not going to budge, Mandy thought, and just

as she was trying to figure out what they could do next — the kitten crept forward.

It was just enough for James to be able to catch hold of him by the scruff of his neck. Mandy saw the kitten go limp as James plucked him off the branch. It was exactly what kittens did when their mothers carried them by the loose skin at the back of their necks.

"Awesome!" said India.

Holding the kitten close to his chest, James crouched down, hooked his free arm around the branch, and eased his legs down until his feet touched the top rung of the ladder.

"Be careful now," said Ernie, gripping the ladder firmly.

Moments later, James was making his way back down, the kitten snuggled against him. Todd didn't even try to struggle. *He must know he's in good hands,* Mandy thought.

On the ground, James handed Todd to India. "One kitten in good condition."

"Thank you, thank you!" she said, hugging the kitten. And then she hugged James, too.

James blushed. "I only climbed the ladder," he protested. "It was Mandy who found him. And Ernie arrived just at the right time, too."

"Pure luck," muttered Ernie.

"We would have struggled without you," said Mandy as she stroked the blossom-covered kitten. She smiled at James. "You were a star."

"Yes, thank you, James," said Mrs. Arquette, putting her hand on his arm. "You took a big risk there."

James blushed even more.

"Let's clean you up, Todd," Mandy said. She began to pick off the sticky blossoms while the kitten cuddled up against his owner.

"I'll be on my way then," said Ernie, picking up the ladder and going toward the gate.

"Oh, don't go yet, Mr . . . er . . ." said Mrs. Arquette.

"Bell. But call me Ernie."

"All right. Ernie," said India's mom. "Thank you very much for your help, Ernie. Won't you stay for a cup of tea? It's the least we can do."

"Another time." Ernie looked down at his stained clothing. "I'm a little grubby."

"That's all right. So am I," said Mrs. Arquette, glancing at her own paint-splattered clothes.

Ernie didn't seem to hear her. "I haven't had time to wash my overalls with all the worry about the goats."

Mandy's thoughts shot back to Lydia and the goats. Todd was safe, but what about Lady Jayne, Alexandra, and Monty? "Are they any better?" she asked Ernie.

"Not that I've heard. But you know what Lydia's like. Won't use that phone of hers unless you force her," said Ernie. "I was just on my way up to the farm, so I'd better get along. I can't have Lydia worrying about me, too." He went through the gate and strapped the ladder onto the roof of his van. "See you all later," he called, climbing into the driver's seat. And with a beep of the horn, he drove off.

"What did he mean about the goats, Mandy?" asked Mrs. Arquette. "Are they the same goats that helped make that lovely hand lotion your mother gave me?"

"Yes. Some of them are very sick, and my dad hasn't discovered what's wrong with them yet."

Mrs. Arquette looked sympathetic. "I am sorry to hear that. When you see Lydia again, would you tell her I hope the goats get well soon?"

"Sure," said Mandy.

Mrs. Arquette stroked Todd's head. "Let's hope you've learned your lesson about climbing trees, you little scamp."

"He was just being a cat," said India.

"Mmm, with a little help from you," said her mom. "You're going to have to be more careful about keeping your door closed in the future. If he gets out again, he might not be so easy to find."

"He won't get out again," muttered India. "Not until

he's old enough." She watched her mom go back into the house. "She's always on my case," she complained when the door closed. "Do this, don't do that," she said in a mocking voice.

"Maybe she's really busy right now," Mandy said. She glanced at James, hoping he'd have something helpful to say. But he shrugged and concentrated on putting on his shoes and socks.

"She wouldn't be so busy if she hadn't changed her job and if Dad still lived with us," said India.

Mandy thought hard. "Well, I guess your mom must have worked it all out. Parents usually have good reasons for doing things, and it doesn't mean that they don't want the best for us and that they don't love us." This was so difficult! Animals were much easier to deal with than people.

India sniffed and cuddled Todd closer. The kitten rubbed his face against her neck, purring.

James straightened up and pushed his glasses up on his nose. "The thing is," he said, and Mandy waited for one of his good ideas. "It's like you said, India. We have to make sure Todd doesn't get out again on his own until he's settled down. We could get him a harness and you could take him out on a leash to get used to his new surroundings."

"That's not a bad idea," Mandy said. "I read that

Burmese cats can be a lot like dogs, and love following their owners around on explorations outside."

"There's no point," said India. She picked a piece of blossom off Todd's ear and flicked it onto the grass. "Mom might as well find a new home for him."

"What?" Mandy gasped.

India shrugged. "Well, I've lost everything else. I can't take care of him the right way, and Mom obviously doesn't want him around."

"But you didn't do anything wrong, and kittens always make trouble," Mandy said.

"Yeah, but Todd eats the wrong things, and now he's got that gin . . . gin — whatever disease . . ."

"No, he doesn't," Mandy said, annoyed with herself for not telling India sooner. "Look, we came around to tell you that Todd doesn't have gingivitis after all."

"He doesn't?"

"No. Mom and Dad say he's probably just teething."

"Well, that's good news," said India, looking a little happier.

Mandy took the toothbrush and paste out of her pocket. "We brought this for you. I'll show you how to clean his teeth so that he never gets gum disease."

"Thanks, Mandy," said India. "It's really nice of you to help like this." Although she sounded relieved, she still seemed upset. "The thing is, I still don't know how I'm going to stop him from getting into trouble. Mom's warned me she can't cope if he does anything else."

"I bet she doesn't really mean it," said James.

"She does. She's fed up and stressed out, and she says Todd's making it worse."

"Then let's make sure Todd *doesn't* make it worse," said Mandy. "You can start by taking him out for walks. If he gets plenty of exercise, he might not cause so much trouble at home."

India shook her head. "It won't make any difference. As soon as school starts, he'll be on his own all day and he'll be even worse." She looked away. "Of course, if Dad were here, everything would be okay. He works at home, so Todd wouldn't get bored."

"Look, why don't we find some ways of keeping Todd busy when you're at school?" suggested Mandy.

"Like what?"

Mandy thought for a moment. "Like, give him some toys." There wasn't a lot Todd could play with in India's room, which is probably why he got his claws into India's clothes. "You know how I said that Burmese were like dogs in some ways?"

India nodded.

"Well, just like you'd leave a puppy with lots of toys,

it might work if you left Todd with things he could play with," Mandy explained.

"He likes to hunt and chase and pounce on things, so let's give him things he can practice on," said James.

"That's a good idea," said India, scratching Todd under his chin. "The trouble is I don't have any cat toys, and I just spent all my allowance on a new lamp shade for my room."

"You don't have to *buy* any," Mandy said. "We can make some."

"Out of all his favorite things, too," said James. "Like satin and pieces of cardboard."

"And a ripped-up T-shirt," said India with a smile.

Mandy chuckled. "I guess we could use it to make something. So, what do you say, India? Should we get started?"

Todd was already struggling in India's arms, wanting to get down. "The sooner the better," said India.

They hurried back in, and after shutting Todd safely in India's room, they scoured the house for some good toy-making materials.

There were still several empty packing boxes in the living room. "Do you mind if we use some of these boxes, Mrs. Arquette?" Mandy asked.

"And this string?" said James, picking up a couple of pieces from the carpet.

"We'll need these scissors too," India added, taking three pairs out of a desk drawer.

"Take what you like. What are you up to?" asked Mrs. Arquette, looking puzzled. She was kneeling on the floor, painting the skirting boards.

"Cat toys," Mandy said. "To keep Todd out of trouble."

"Good idea!" said Mrs. Arquette. "We should have thought of that before."

Ten minutes later, they were back in India's room, surrounded by pieces of string, the satin from the old box of candy hearts, the cardboard tube from a toilet-paper roll, a couple of cardboard boxes, a bottle of glue, scissors, crayons, and various other things that had been destined for the garbage.

"I'll start with the toilet roll," said India, sitting on the floor with her legs folded beneath her. "And some satin."

"I'll take some of that satin, too," said James. "And I need a long piece of string."

Todd was play-fighting with the teddy bear on the bed. He gripped it in his front paws and kicked it with his strong back legs.

"Soon you'll have a lot more to play with," Mandy told him.

Todd gripped the teddy tightly and peered at Mandy. There was a mischievous glint in his eyes, and his tail swished from side to side. Suddenly, he sprang up and leaped off the bed, diving into one of the cardboard boxes.

"Hey! I know what I'll make," Mandy said. She sat down on the floor, cross-legged, and pulled the other box onto her lap. Todd tried to spring onto her knees, colliding with the box. "Not yet," Mandy said. "Play with this instead." She rolled a pencil across the carpet. Todd chased after it, pushing it under the bed. He flattened himself on the floor and poked his paw after it.

"That should keep him busy for a few minutes," Mandy said. "Pass me those scissors please, James."

He gave them to her and she began cutting a rectangular shape out of the side of the box. Within a few minutes, her project began taking shape.

"It's a little house!" said India. "Todd's going to love it."

"I hope so," Mandy said, taping curtains made from the ruined T-shirt over the windows — two square holes she'd cut on either side of the rectangular door. There was even a chimney stuck to the flat roof, which was actually the bottom of the box.

"It just needs a name now," Mandy said, choosing a red felt-tip pen from India's pencil case.

"Todd's Place?" suggested James, tying a strip of satin to the string.

Nearby, Todd had given up trying to hook the pencil out from under the bed. He'd found a small roll of sticky tape and was flicking it around in front of him.

"How about Todd's Den?" said India.

"That's perfect," said Mandy. She wrote the name above the door in big capital letters. "Let's see what Todd thinks of it."

Todd came over and sniffed the box before going inside. A second later, one of the curtains twitched and Todd's chocolate brown face appeared at the window. He looked at Mandy and meowed. Then he started to bite the cardboard windowsill.

"I guess he approves," Mandy said, feeling pleased.

"Here, Todd. Do you like this, too?" James held up a long piece of string with red satin bows tied along it. He fastened it to the back of a chair so that it dangled down, reaching almost to the ground. James flicked it.

Todd dashed out from his den and batted the string so that it swung wildly. He stood up on his hind legs and grabbed one of the bows in his claws. Soon he was swinging on the string as it twisted around and around with him clinging to it like an acrobat.

"I didn't mean for it to be a climbing rope." James laughed. "But if that's what he wants it to be, why not?"

"I hope he doesn't get dizzy or sick," said India.

"Did he get sick again?" Mandy asked.

"Just once, last night. After I caught him chewing up some newspaper. It must have tasted yucky."

"Probably," Mandy said.

India held something up. "What do you think of this?"

It was the toilet-paper tube covered in red satin, with a tiny bell attached inside. India rolled it over the carpet. The musical tinkling of the bell distracted Todd. He let go of his string and bounded after the new toy. It came to a stop and he stopped, too. He dabbed at it suspiciously with one paw and it moved an inch. He pawed it again, this time hard enough that it rolled away, jingling like a sleigh.

Todd raced after it, batting it in front of him. It rolled into his den. He dove in after it. A few thuds later, it flew out of the door. And Todd shot out after it.

"It's like he's got his own adventure playground," said India.

Mandy grinned. "Well, let's hope it keeps him busy!"

Mandy was helping Jean Knox with some filing the next morning when a white delivery van came up the driveway. On the side were the words, WALTON PATHOLOGICAL LABORATORY. Mandy's heart started to pound. "It must be the blood test results," she said.

The driver came inside, holding an envelope. "Special delivery," he said, handing it to Mandy.

It had to be bad news. Why else would the lab have sent the results so quickly, by special delivery rather than ordinary mail?

Mandy took the envelope to her dad in his treatment room.

"Ah. The foot-and-mouth results." Dr. Adam tore open the envelope and studied the report inside.

Mandy's mom came in. "Well?"

"Well, it's not foot-and-mouth," said Dr. Adam.

Mandy wanted to cheer!

"And it's none of the other conditions I tested for. So, according to this," Dr. Adam waved the sheet of paper, "there's nothing wrong with the goats. Unless . . ."

Mandy guessed what he wasn't saying. "Unless it's scrapie," she whispered. She could hardly bear to think about what this meant. There would have to be a diagnosis, of course, but that would mean . . . she tried to push it from her mind. "What do we do now?"

"We'll have to tell Lydia," said her dad, folding up the report. "Let's go up to the farm. We're not expecting any patients until this afternoon."

Leaving Jean and Simon, the veterinary nurse, to hold down the fort, Mandy and her parents drove up to High Cross Farm. It was a cold, cloudy day and there were still traces of last night's frost on the ground.

Ernie's van was parked in the paved yard. Climbing

out of the Land Rover, Mandy caught a glimpse of Ernie in the field behind the barn where she'd seen Houdini the other day. Heavily dressed against the cold, Ernie was sweeping his paintbrush up and down the fence posts. Mandy tried to see if Houdini was there, too, but there was no sign of him.

Lydia hurried over from the quarantine barn. "I'm so glad you're here," she said. "I was just going to call you."

She looked agitated and her voice was breathless. Did this mean the goats were worse? Mandy braced herself for more bad news.

"You're not going to believe this," said Lydia. "But Lady Jayne, Monty, and Alexandra are better!"

"Better!" Mandy and her parents looked at Lydia and then at one another in amazement.

"Yes. I thought they seemed happier last night, but I told myself it was wishful thinking," said Lydia. "But I just spent half an hour with them now and they're as right as rain. No scratching, no drooling, no circling — nothing."

Mandy felt as if the weight of the world had been lifted from her shoulders. "That's great news! It means they don't have scrapie!"

"If they're better, that's right," said her mom. But she and Dr. Adam looked mystified.

"We'll have to examine them again," said Mandy's dad, "just to make sure all's well."

"Come on, then," said Lydia happily and she led the way back to the quarantine barn.

Monty, Alexandra, and Lady Jayne trotted over to say hello as soon as Mandy and her parents came in. They nickered with excitement as Mandy pulled out some apple slices for them.

Mandy's parents checked the three goats, taking their temperatures, listening to their hearts and examining their mouths, noses, and feet. "All clear, that's for sure," said Dr. Adam when he'd finished looking at Alexandra. "You were right the other day, Mandy, when you said they might recover on their own like Jemima did. But whatever was wrong with them is still a big mystery."

Lydia nodded. "But the main thing is that they're well again. I'm sorry you came all the way up here for nothing."

Mandy paused to give each goat an affectionate pat before following her parents and Lydia outside again. "You're quite a bunch," she said, glancing back at the goats from the door, "getting better all on your own like that."

Out in the yard, she heard Ernie calling out.

"Lydia!" He appeared at the fence, a paintbrush in his hand. A thick black substance was dripping off the brush onto the ground. "Houdini's getting into a stew in the barn. I can hear him kicking against his stall. Should we let him out?"

"Okay. But don't get mad if he gets in your way," Lydia replied. "It's difficult to keep that goat in, even on cold days," she said to the Hopes. "He got used to coming out while Ernie's been working in the barn. But most of the pens are done, so I was going to keep him indoors until the weather starts warming up."

"He's obviously got a different plan," said Dr. Emily.

"I'll go get him," Mandy offered.

"Thanks, dear," said Lydia.

Mandy could hear Houdini kicking the wooden sides of his stall even before she entered the barn. She was surprised at how forceful the kicking sounded. Even though Houdini regularly escaped, it was usually because he'd climbed out of his pen or a field. He didn't normally try to break his way out.

"Coming, Houdini!" she called, half-running down the walkway. There was a strong smell of the stuff Ernie was using to treat the wood. She opened the gate to Houdini's pen, then stopped abruptly. "Oh, no!"

Houdini was standing against one wall. His head drooped and he was scratching himself frantically as if his skin was crawling with mites. His leg kept banging hard against the wooden panels, sending whirls of dust into the air.

"Not you, too, Houdini," Mandy said. She felt an ice-cold shiver run down her spine. The mystery symptoms hadn't gone away — they'd just shifted to a different goat. And even worse than before by the look of him.

Houdini lifted his head and looked at Mandy.

"No!" She gasped.

Blood was streaming from his nose.

Nine

Mandy burst into the kitchen. "Come quickly! Houdini's bleeding!"

Mandy's parents flew into action. They pulled on rubber gloves and ran out to the pen to examine the distressed goat. Mandy stood close by, ready to do anything she could to help.

"Flashlight, please," said Dr. Adam. He was holding Houdini's head in both hands, dabbing at the blood on his nose with a swab.

Mandy took the light out of the vet's bag and gave it to her father. He switched it on and shone it into Houdini's nostrils.

"Thermometer," said Dr. Emily.

Lydia and Ernie were outside the pen. Lydia's expression was blank as she watched what was happening. But knowing Lydia, Mandy knew she was churned up inside. Ernie was frowning so deeply, his thick white eyebrows almost met in the middle.

"Normal temperature," said Dr. Emily, giving the thermometer back to Mandy.

"I can't see what's causing this nosebleed," said Dr. Adam. He shone the flashlight into Houdini's eyes.

"What are you looking for?" Mandy asked.

"Just checking his reflexes."

Houdini pulled his head away from Dr. Adam and bleated angrily.

"Sorry, old boy," said Dr. Adam. "Give me a hand, Mandy."

She put her arm around the goat's neck, holding him firmly but not so tightly that he'd be uncomfortable. With her other hand, she stroked the top of his head. "Keep still just a little longer."

Houdini grew calmer.

"Good job, Mandy," said her dad, and he peered into the goat's dark eyes. He switched off the light and straightened up. "Beats me," he said to his wife. "Nothing obviously wrong. And he's still as strong as an ox."

"Yes. He's okay, but not okay," said Dr. Emily.

"Maybe he's eaten something he shouldn't have," Mandy said. But except for rhododendron leaves, Houdini seemed to have a cast-iron stomach. Windshield wipers, flower pots — he'd munched his way through them without any bad aftereffects.

Dr. Emily glanced around the stall. "Poisoning did cross my mind. But nothing in here would have done it. And he's been in for a while, hasn't he, Lydia?"

"Since yesterday morning after Ernie finished his pen."

Dr. Adam watched the goat rub himself against the fence. "Let's take him into the daylight so we can really check his skin."

Outside, a weak sun was trying to come out from behind the clouds. Houdini sniffed the air. He seemed glad to be outdoors again. They went into the fenced-off field behind the barn where Ernie had been working earlier. His sticky paint can was on the ground just inside the gate. Houdini bent down to investigate it, and Ernie quickly scooped it up. "No, you don't. Not again." He balanced it on top of a fence post. "He kicked it over yesterday when I was putting him back in his pen. I had to put fresh straw all over the place."

"You'd think the smell alone would stop him from going near it," said Mandy.

"I know what you mean," said Lydia, but Mandy

hardly heard her. *Paint can, kicked it over, back in his pen, yesterday . . . what did it all mean?* She stroked Houdini's back, trying to make sense of the half thoughts filling her head.

Mandy's parents were examining Houdini's skin. Ernie put his arm around Lydia as if to comfort her, but she pushed him away. "Don't. That wood treatment is all over your clothes. The smell gives me a headache."

Mandy looked at Lydia. *The smell gives me a headache.* Could the goats be reacting to the sticky black wood treatment that Ernie had painted all over their barn?

"I still can't rule out scrapie," Dr. Adam was saying. Mandy was so deep in thought, her dad's voice sounded like it was in a tunnel. "We know the disease develops slowly and can last for months. But the baffling part is that the others have gotten better . . ."

"But that's just it," Mandy said, as everything began to fall into place. "The others got better. It was like they were allergic to something, and then they weren't exposed to it anymore." She pointed to the paint can. "That stuff, maybe."

Everyone looked at the can, and back to Mandy. There was a glimmer of hope in Lydia's eyes, but she didn't say anything. She turned to the two vets and waited.

"You might just have a point, Mandy," said Dr. Adam. He went to the can and studied the label. It was almost blotted out by the black goo that had dripped down the sides. "This is the original can, isn't it, Ernie? I mean, you haven't poured that stuff into this can?"

"No. I bought it years ago, when I was still working. It's been in my shed ever since."

Dr. Adam screwed up his eyes, trying to make out what was on the label.

Mandy went to see if she could read it. "'Contains Creo' — something." The rest of the word, as well as the list of the other ingredients were covered with a black blob.

"Creosote poisoning!" Dr. Emily looked at Dr. Adam. "Wouldn't you agree?"

Mandy's dad nodded. "Absolutely. The symptoms are typical of it. Why didn't we think of it earlier?"

Lydia spun around and glared at Ernie. "You've poisoned my goats, you old fool."

Ernie shrugged helplessly. "I didn't know it would hurt them, I promise."

"First Jemima became ill after you'd painted her stall," Lydia went on. "She got better when we put her in an untreated pen." She spoke faster and faster, like a train gathering speed. "It was after you treated the wood in the other stalls that the rest of the goats developed the symptoms. But they recovered quickly after we put them in the old barn. And now Houdini has reacted."

A loud bleat from Houdini sounded strangely like a nasal *yes*.

"Houdini's had it the worst and that's because you let him kick the tin over, Ernie," Lydia said accusingly.

"I didn't *let* him," said Ernie. "He chose to. That goat's his own master."

"You know you should keep things out of his way."

"And you know it's not always easy." Ernie found the lid of the can and banged it back into place. "Anyway, how was I to know the goats would react badly? I used gallons of this stuff while I was in business. I never had any complaints."

"Probably because you never worked around goats," said Lydia.

With his head down, Ernie headed for the gate. "I'm sorry, Lydia. You know I'd never harm the goats on purpose."

Lydia didn't say anything but just kept stroking Houdini.

Mandy was feeling very sorry for Ernie. "It's been horrible for everyone," she said. "But at least we know what's going on now. And we know that Houdini will be all right, just like Jemima and the others."

"And it's no one's fault, really," said Dr. Adam. "Creosote is nasty stuff. That's why you can't buy it in stores anymore."

Ernie paused at the gate and looked back. "I didn't know that."

"You wouldn't have," said Dr. Emily, "since you haven't bought any for years."

"Yeah," said Ernie, but he still looked very dejected.

"What now?" said Lydia. "Is there any treatment? I mean, Houdini's got it the worst, hasn't he? He might take longer to get better."

"I can give him an antihistamine to calm the allergic reaction," said Dr. Emily, pulling off her rubber gloves. "And it won't hurt to give it to all the others, too. I'll go back to Animal Ark and get the medication right away."

Dr. Adam peeled off his rubber gloves, too. It was a welcome sign to Mandy. *No more risk of a deadly disease.*

"You'll have to keep the herd somewhere else for now, Lydia," said Dr. Adam, stuffing the gloves into his pocket. "Until the creosote is stripped off the wood."

Ernie looked startled. "Strip it all off?"

Dr. Adam nodded. "It's a shame about your hard work, but it's the only way."

"I'll help," Mandy offered. "I bet James will too."

"I'm not bothered by hard work," said Ernie. "Work never frightened me. But the thing is, we can't take the stuff off. It soaked right into the wood."

Lydia's face darkened. "Don't tell me that, Ernie. If that stuff can't come off, we're going to have to get new poles, new fencing panels for the stalls. . . . It'll cost a fortune!"

"All the goats are squashed in that old barn," Mandy said to James a few hours later. She was at his house, bringing him up to date with the situation at High Cross Farm.

"It's great that they haven't got a serious disease," said James. "But it must be like a madhouse in that tiny barn."

"It is. But Lydia doesn't know what else to do with them," Mandy said. "They can't go outside because the forecast is for snow."

"There's got to be a way to make the big barn safe again," said James. He was at his computer, doing some research on the Internet for a school science project. "Let's see what we can find on the web."

Mandy pulled up a chair next to him. She watched him type CREOSOTE+BARN+DIY into the search menu. A page came up with a long list of topics. James scrolled through them. "Nothing much here."

He was about to click the mouse to start another search when Mandy saw a topic at the bottom of the list. RAISING SHEEP IN MY OWN DIY BARN. Beneath this was a web address, www.chad'ssheepblog. danvilleschool.com

"Let's see what that's about," she said.

The site turned out to be an online diary belonging to a high school pupil, Chad Abrahams. He lived in a farm community in the state of Virginia and he was raising sheep for a school project. He'd even built his own barn, with the help of his dad and older brother.

The blog showed a picture of Chad, stocky and dark-haired with an open, friendly face. He was carrying a tiny, snow-white lamb that looked as if it had just been born. Another image showed him in the middle of a small flock of sheep. There was a sheepdog lying nearby, his sharp gaze fixed on his master. A caption with an arrow pointing to the dog read, MY TRUSTY CO-SHEPHERD, STREAK.

"Hey, look at that," Mandy said when James clicked to the next page. There was a photograph of a wooden barn with Chad standing at the door, a box of tools on the ground next to him. The caption read, MY MULTI-PURPOSE BARN: SHEEP HOME/SHEEP-SHEARING STATION/ WOOL SHED!"

Mandy was intrigued. "Let's e-mail him. If he built a barn, he might know something about creosote."

James clicked on a box that said CONTACT ME. A blank

e-mail window appeared on the screen. James typed, HI, CHAD, COOL BLOG!

Mandy pushed James's hands off the keyboard and typed, AND COOL DOG!

"Trust you to focus on the dog," said James. He continued to type, giving the details of the creosote problem at High Cross Farm. "WE'VE GOT TO FIND A WAY OF GETTING THE CREOSOTE OFF THE WOOD. ANY IDEAS?"

"Let's keep our fingers crossed," Mandy said as James clicked on SEND.

They went to have lunch — cheese-and-tomato sandwiches and orange juice that James prepared because his mom was out for the day. They raced through it, wanting to get back to the computer quickly and see if there was a reply.

There *was* a reply! HEY, MANDY AND JAMES. I JUST GOT TO SCHOOL AND SAW YOUR E-MAIL. IT'S GREAT TO HEAR FROM YOU! Chad's message began.

"He sounds like a really friendly guy," said James.

"Yep," Mandy agreed, scanning the message. "And exactly the person we needed because there's the answer."

A FARMER ACROSS THE VALLEY HAD THE SAME PROBLEM ONCE. HIS SHEEP WERE REALLY SICK, SO HE PAINTED OVER THE CREOSOTE WITH RESIN, WHICH IS LIKE THICK, TRANSPARENT

PAINT. I THINK IT WAS CALLED WOODSEAL. THAT DID THE
TRICK. THE SHEEP GOT BETTER FAST. I HOPE THIS HELPS. LET
ME KNOW.

Mandy didn't waste a second. She picked up the
phone and dialed Lydia's number.

Early the next morning, Mandy and James were back at
the farm. James had borrowed his dad's digital camera.
He was going to take photographs of their work and
e-mail them to Chad that evening.

India was there, too. When Mandy called to ask about
Todd, she'd told India about the drama with the goats.
India had immediately volunteered to help. "Ernie
helped with Todd, so I owe him a favor," she said. "And
Todd should be all right on his own in his adventure
park for a few hours."

Hurrying across the yard to the main barn, Mandy
glanced over at the dilapidated one. She was tempted
to go and see how the goats were. But the creosote-
covering job was more urgent. Houdini and the others,
squashed in their temporary quarters, would agree.

They found Ernie busy at work already. He must have
been at the hardware store in Walton the moment it
opened that morning to buy the resin.

"I'm glad you had the sense to dress properly," he
said, looking them up and down.

They were all wearing old clothes — frayed and faded jeans and sweat suit tops. "There's a paintbrush for each of you," he went on, "and a can of Woodseal."

They each chose an enclosure and started to work. The transparent resin was very sticky, but nothing like the thick black goo that had soaked into the wood. And best of all, it didn't have a strong smell.

They'd made good progress, and James had taken lots of photographs, when Lydia came to join them twenty minutes later. She was scruffier than ever in a baggy pair of khaki overalls. The sleeves and legs were so long she'd rolled them up then tied string around them at her ankles and wrists. She was definitely at her most unglamorous, yet Mandy noticed Ernie's expression soften when she came in.

"Morning, everyone," she called. She shook her head when James lifted the camera to take a picture of her. "You can photograph the goats, but not me." She noticed India working on a pen near the far end of the barn. "You must be India."

India nodded. "Hi, Ms. Fawcett. I love your goats. They're almost as gorgeous as my kitten Todd."

"They probably get in a lot more trouble, though," said Lydia.

"I don't know," said India. Mandy thought she saw a shadow cross her face. "I just hope Todd manages to be

good while I'm here," she went on. "Mom's still a little uptight about him."

"I'm sure he will. He's got all his toys," Mandy said. "How's Houdini today, Lydia?"

"Coming along," she replied, dipping a paintbrush in a pot of resin.

"And the other goats?" James prompted.

Lydia glanced at Ernie sideways. "Cramped. And milking them was just horrible. Like trying to do wood-work with a straitjacket on."

Mandy saw Ernie sigh.

"You might as well sigh, Ernie Bell," grumbled Lydia. "The work you've caused me!"

"Yeah," muttered the old man, sweeping his paint-brush up and down a wooden panel.

They worked for several hours solid. Mandy noticed Lydia glance at Ernie every few minutes. She kept talk-ing to herself, too, saying things like, "Nothing but trouble. Whole lot of good, a fiancé. Fine on our own, me and the goats."

Poor Ernie, Mandy thought. *He was only trying to help.*

At last, just before midday, every inch of creosote-soaked wood in the barn was covered in shiny resin. The place was sparkling and there wasn't even a linger-ing whiff of creosote.

"All done," said Ernie, rubbing his hands.

Lydia was looking through the door, "And just in time. It's starting to snow."

A flurry of snowflakes drifted down, melting as soon as they touched the ground.

"I bet the goats can't wait to get back in here," Mandy said. "Should we bring them across?"

"Soon," said Lydia. "We need a drink first. That was thirsty work."

Their clothes were covered in sticky resin so they stayed in the barn while Lydia got some refreshments. She returned carrying a tray full of steaming mugs of hot chocolate, and, to Mandy's dismay, a plate of the goat's milk fudge.

"I expect you'd prefer coffee to hot chocolate," said Lydia, giving Ernie one of the mugs.

"No, no. I love hot chocolate, my dear."

Mandy smiled to herself. Poor Ernie. He was probably dead scared of saying or doing something that might upset Lydia further.

They were still enjoying their hard-earned snack when Lydia stood up. Without a word, she left the barn. A minute later, Ernie went outside, too.

"Now what?" Mandy asked the others.

"Do you think they're having a fight?" said James. He helped himself to a piece of fudge and popped it into his mouth. The look of shock on his face caused Mandy to nearly burst out laughing. "Yuck!" James exclaimed after he'd swallowed the fudge.

India didn't seem to notice James's reaction. "I hate it when grown-ups argue," she said, chewing her thumbnail.

Mandy guessed she was thinking about her parents. "Ernie and Lydia can't be having an argument," she said. "The crisis is over. And just look at this place." She waved her hand around the barn. "It never looked so good."

"Yes, indeed," said Lydia, returning just then. Her hands were behind her back as if she was hiding something. She looked around, frowning. "Where's Ernie?"

"He followed you out," said James. "Didn't you see him?"

Lydia shook her head and sat down on a bale of hay just as Ernie returned. He was holding *his* hands behind his back, too. "Lydia, my dear," he began. His frown was so exaggerated that Mandy felt nervous about what he was about to say. Perhaps, after all the strain of the last few days and Lydia being so angry with him, he was going to break off the engagement.

"I'm very, very sorry about causing the goats harm," he went on.

Lydia sat up straight. "You didn't mean to do it."

Ernie blinked. "I have something for you."

"Me, too," said Lydia.

At exactly the same moment, they brought their hands out from behind their backs. They were each holding a box of Mrs. McFarlane's chocolate hearts!

As they all roared with laughter, Mandy became aware of someone else joining in. Except that it wasn't laughter she heard, but bleating. She looked around. A goat as black as tar with eyes like sparkling black diamonds was standing in the doorway. "Houdini! How did you get in here?"

Not that it mattered. What was most important, as far as Mandy was concerned, was how well Houdini was looking. He trotted through the door, his head held high. As soon as he saw the boxes of candies, he went straight for them.

"Watch out!" Mandy warned, and Lydia quickly grabbed both boxes and shoved them inside her overcoat.

Houdini stopped, looking very indignant.

"They're not for you," Lydia told him. "Goats don't celebrate Valentine's Day."

Houdini bleated again.

"Maybe he thinks he deserves a Valentine's gift, too," Mandy said, laughing.

Ten

"Wasn't that awesome, the way Ernie and Lydia surprised each other with the candy hearts?" Mandy asked, watching Ernie's van turn the corner at the end of Playground Lane. He'd dropped them all off at India's house, after a bumpy and rather uncomfortable ride down from the farm. Mandy and James had ridden in the back, among the paint cans and other equipment. India had sat in front with Ernie. As owners of kittens, they had a lot in common.

"It was so cool," India agreed.

Mrs. Arquette was in the kitchen, putting a casserole in the oven.

"Is that for lunch?" asked India.

Mrs. Arquette closed the oven. "Sorry, dear, no," she said, taking off her oven mitts. "It's vegetable moussaka for when your father comes to dinner tomorrow night."

India turned to Mandy and James and gave them a thumbs-up.

Mandy felt her heart sink. It looked as if India still had high hopes for Valentine's Day.

Mrs. Arquette started slicing a loaf of bread. "You all must be hungry after your hard work."

"Starving!" said James.

Mrs. Arquette smiled. "I'll have lunch ready in two seconds."

"We'll just go up to see Todd," said India. "I hope he hasn't been too lonely. Or bad."

"He's been fine," said her mom, spreading butter on a slice of bread.

India gave a sigh of relief.

"I brought him down while I was having coffee earlier," her mom went on. "He scooted around with his toys, and when he was tired, he went to sleep on my lap."

"See, Mom," said India, looking even more relieved. "He's an angel!"

"That's a matter of opinion," said Mrs. Arquette. "It was a good idea to make those toys, and I know you're looking after him carefully and spending as much time as you can with him. But left on his own, who knows what he might do?"

And what has he been doing since Mrs. Arquette put him back in India's room? Mandy wondered on the way upstairs. Was he still playing with his toys, or was the novelty beginning to wear off?

A quick glance round the room revealed that nothing was out of order: no ripped-up paper, no broken items, no chewed-up clothes or cushions.

No Todd either!

Mandy went cold. James murmured, "Not again."

India didn't look at all troubled. "I know exactly where he is," she said, and she crouched down in front of Todd's Den.

Mandy and James knelt down beside her and peeped in through the cutout door. Sure enough, Todd was there, curled up in the candy box.

"That's his favorite bed," India explained.

"And he's the perfect replacement for the chocolates," Mandy joked. It was one of the sweetest things she'd seen in a long time. "You've got to take a picture, James."

James took several shots of the sleeping kitten. He showed them to Mandy and India in the view window on the camera.

Mandy loved them all. With his sleek chocolate-colored coat, Todd looked stunning against the red satin fabric.

"They're great photos," said India. "Like the pictures you see on the lids of boxes of candy."

"Hear that, Todd? You're a real candy-box kitten," Mandy said.

"I'll print them out for you," James promised India. "And if you like, we can get some enlarged so you can frame them for your room."

"That would be nice," said India, and added wistfully, "just in case Mom won't let me keep him."

Mandy and James looked at each other but said nothing.

Leaving Todd sleeping, they went back downstairs for lunch. Outside, it was snowing steadily.

"We'd better go before it gets any deeper," said James, after he and Mandy had helped to clear up.

"We'll see you at school, India," Mandy said. The winter break was almost over; school started again in two days.

"If not before," said Mrs. Arquette. "Now that I've nearly finished getting the house together, it would be nice if you and your parents could join us for a house-warming dinner tomorrow."

"But it's Valentine's Day!" said India.

Her mom looked surprised. "Oh, yes, so it is. I'd

completely forgotten. Have your parents already made plans, Mandy?"

"Uh, no, I don't think so," Mandy said.

India rushed out of the kitchen, letting the door slam shut behind her. Mrs. Arquette raised her eyebrows, but Mandy knew exactly what was wrong.

India's hopes had been shattered. Her mom wasn't planning a romantic Valentine's dinner with her dad after all. She hadn't even remembered what day it was!

Mandy felt nervous when she and her parents arrived at the Arquettes' house the following evening. How would India cope with visitors when all she wanted was for her mom and dad to be on their own?

India opened the door to let them in. She looked bright-eyed and excited, and she was wearing a fluffy red sweater over a pair of new jeans. "Come and meet my dad!" she said. She led them to the living room, which had been totally transformed since the last time Mandy had seen it. There were no more packing boxes or crumpled-up newspapers littering the floor; instead, the knickknacks were arranged on the mantelpiece and the books were neatly packed on the bookshelves.

Mr. Arquette had the same thick auburn hair and green eyes as India. Casually dressed in black jeans and a brown sweater, he was sitting on the floor, playing with Todd.

He jumped up when the Hopes came in, picking up the kitten as he did.

"Dad, this is Mandy, and her mom and dad," said India.

"It's great to meet you," he said, shaking Dr. Adam's hand. "I've heard so much about you all."

"And India's told us a lot about you, too," said Mandy.

"Good things, I hope." Mr. Arquette smiled, stroking Todd.

Mrs. Arquette came in with a tray of drinks. James was following her, carrying a plate of olives.

"I didn't know you were here already," Mandy said, wondering where Mr. and Mrs. Hunter were.

"I dropped a hint to Dad about it being Valentine's Day," said James. "So he took Mom to that new French restaurant in Walton. They dropped me off on their way."

Mandy noticed a look of sadness cross India's face. *Poor India. I bet she wishes her parents were going out on their own, too.*

Luckily though, Todd was there to cheer her up. India had brought down his toys, and for the next ten minutes, the Burmese kitten kept everyone entertained.

"He's putting that teddy bear to good use," said

Mr. Arquette when Todd pounced on it and gripped it in his paws.

"Yes, but look what he does with this," said India. She rolled the jingling satin-covered tube across the floor.

Todd let go of the teddy bear at once. He crouched low on the ground, his tail swishing, and concentrated on the rolling, musical toy. At exactly the right moment, he sprang forward and caught the cardboard roll in his front paws.

"He's so fast!" said Mr. Arquette.

"I knew you'd love him," said India. She glanced at her mom who was sitting in a chair opposite India and her dad, sipping her drink.

Mrs. Arquette had been watching Todd play but hadn't said anything. As he let go of the cardboard tube and clambered up the side of an armchair, his claws catching the fabric, she narrowed her eyes and frowned. "Don't let him scratch the furniture, India."

Mandy was sitting only a few inches from where Todd was. She leaned over, unhooked his claws and put him on the floor again.

"Sorry, Mom," said India. She shot Mandy a grateful look.

"Here. This is much more fun, little guy," said Mr. Arquette, pulling the satin bow string along the floor.

Todd scampered after it.

"These toys certainly are a big hit," said Mr. Arquette when Todd caught hold of one of the bows.

"He was really bored before we made them," said India.

"Well, he's very busy now. And the picture of health," said Dr. Adam, putting his glass on the coffee table.

"That he is," agreed Dr. Emily. She wriggled her foot and the kitten pounced on it. "I assume he hasn't been sick again."

"Not as far as I know," said Mrs. Arquette. She looked at India. "Has he been sick?"

"Not since he stopped tearing things up so much."

"What sort of things did he tear up?" asked Dr. Emily.

India thought for a moment. "Paper and cardboard and clothes. He chewed a big hole in my best T-shirt."

"Satin, too," said James, handing around a bowl of chips. "He loves shredding satin, doesn't he, India?"

"Satin?" Mrs. Arquette looked appalled. "He hasn't shredded my pajamas, has he, India?"

"No. Nothing like that." India glared at James. He'd nearly given away her secret about buying the expensive chocolates for her mom and dad.

Not that it matters anymore, Mandy thought, *seeing as the candy heart box was ruined*. She noticed that her mom seemed especially thoughtful.

"The first time you brought him to Animal Ark," said

Mandy's mom, "you mentioned he'd thrown up tissue paper and cardboard. And Mandy says he can be very destructive, especially toward newspaper."

Mr. Arquette leaned back on the sofa and put his hands behind his head. "What's wrong with a little paper shredding? It's normal, isn't it? I mean, kittens, puppies, they're demolition experts for a few weeks, but they soon settle down."

India's mom raised her eyebrows. "You have no idea, do you, Martin? Todd has been unbelievably troublesome."

Mandy was afraid India's parents would start arguing in front of them. India looked equally worried.

"You're absolutely right, Alexis," Mr. Arquette replied. "I know I'm too laid back for my own good. But we can't all be organized and in control of things."

Mrs. Arquette stood up to collect the empty glasses.

An uneasy silence followed. Dr. Emily broke it. "I don't think Todd means to be bad." She picked up the kitten, who wanted to climb onto her chair and had decided that the best way was to use her legs as a ladder. "And I'm afraid it's not normal for kittens to eat fabric and other materials." She held Todd up in front of her and studied him. "What's been the problem, little one, hmm?" She turned to Adam Hope. "I'd say pica, wouldn't you?"

"Sounds like it."

India went pale. "What's pica?"

It was a new term to Mandy as well, and to James, judging by his puzzled expression. Mandy felt the knot form in her tummy all over again. Was there more bad news for India?

"Pica is a psychological condition in animals," Dr. Emily explained. "It's a craving for substances the animal wouldn't usually eat, like fabric and paper."

India looked even more alarmed. "Are you saying that Todd's gone crazy?"

"Not at all," said Dr. Adam. He took the kitten from Mandy's mom and cast an expert eye over him while he smoothed his silky coat. "Like we said earlier, he's in great shape. But things like stress, anxiety, boredom, not being able to hunt, sudden changes — like moving to a new home — and even an overdependence on its owner can cause an animal to develop pica."

It all made absolute sense to Mandy. Todd definitely fit the bill when it came to the things her dad had just listed.

India still looked horrified. "You mean he's always going to eat things that are bad for him?"

Before Mandy's parents could answer India, Mrs. Arquette spoke up. "I think you've put your finger on the problem, Adam," she said. She'd just taken Mr.

Arquette's empty glass from him. Still holding the glass, she looked at him and then at India.

India shot a desperate glance at Mandy. Was Mrs. Arquette about to say that because Todd had a problem, he'd have to go to a new home? Mandy looked back helplessly at India.

Mrs. Arquette went on. "It *has* been a difficult few months . . ." she paused and then continued, ". . . for all of us. So it's not surprising Todd has developed pica."

Mandy held her breath.

"But he hasn't been too bad in the last couple of days," she went on. "And you've been very good at taking care of him lately, India. I'm sure he must be getting over his problems."

Mandy closed her eyes as a feeling of relief washed over her. When she opened them, she saw the color had returned to India's cheeks.

"You mean I can keep him?" said India.

"Of course," said her mom, looking surprised. "I never dreamed we'd have to find him another home. We just need to give ourselves a chance to settle in, that's all."

"Magic!" James exclaimed, then blushed when everyone looked at him. "I mean, I'm glad our toys did the trick."

Mrs. Arquette put the glass on the tray and headed for the door. "Now, before we *all* start eating unusual substances due to starvation," she said, "let's have dinner."

The dining room table was covered in a crisp white cloth. There was an arrangement of yellow flowers in the center and two tall white candles on either side of it. Shiny silver cutlery flanked the cream-colored mats at each place. There wasn't even a hint that it was Valentine's Day.

India helped her mom to bring out the first course, homemade tomato soup and toasted French bread. Mandy had brought Todd's toys in to make sure he didn't get into any mischief while they were eating. She dangled the satin-bow string; Todd caught it at once and looked up at Mandy, blinking. "Good boy," she said, tugging the string.

With surprising strength, the little Burmese pulled it right out of her hands. It landed in a heap next to him. He picked one end up in his mouth and for a second, Mandy thought he was about to eat it. "No —" she began, but Todd was already rolling over and over, tying himself up in the string.

"A kitten package." Mr. Arquette smiled. "It's a shame I won't get to see him too often. He's a great character."

"You can see him whenever you like," said India. "Especially if you came to live here."

Her dad shook his head. "The thing is, India," he put

his arm around her shoulder, "I've gone into business with someone in Kent. So I'm going to have to move there."

India looked shattered. Mandy felt terribly sorry for her. Kent was a long way away, down in the southeast corner of England.

"Kent!" India gasped. "That's hundreds of miles away. It's closer to France than to us."

"Well then, isn't that a bonus?" said Mr. Arquette. "When you spend weekends and vacations with me, we can hop over. We'll go to Paris in the spring, the Riviera in summer, Provence in autumn, and the French Alps in winter."

"Sounds marvelous," said Dr. Emily. "I'm envious already."

India bit her lip. "But what about Todd?"

Mandy knew what she meant. Who would look after Todd while she was staying with her dad?

India's mom reached across and touched her arm.

Mandy waited breathlessly for the bad news. *She's changed her mind now that India will be away so much. She's going to tell India that Todd can't stay after all.*

"Don't worry about Todd," said Mrs. Arquette. "I'll take good care of him when you're away."

"You will?" India asked excitedly.

"And to make sure he doesn't get into trouble when we're both at school, I've bought him a little present." Mrs. Arquette got up and left the room.

"Oh! That reminds me," said Mr. Arquette, following her. "I've got something for him as well."

Mandy had a surprise for India of her own — a blown-up version of one of the photos of Todd that James had taken the other day. She was about to get it from the living room where she'd left it, when Mr. and Mrs. Arquette came back in, their hands behind their backs.

Mandy and James smiled at each other. "Look familiar?" asked James. But somehow, Mandy didn't think India's parents were holding heart-shaped boxes of candy behind their backs.

"I thought this would keep Todd occupied," said Mr. Arquette. He brought his hands out from behind his back.

With a flourish, and exactly at the same time, Mrs. Arquette did, too. "This should make a difference," she said.

Mr. Arquette's gift was a bag of cat treats and an activity ball. It was hollow so that it could be filled with the treats. "He can chase it all over the house getting the goodies to fall out."

"It's perfect," said India. "I can't wait to see him play with it."

Mrs. Arquette was holding a square-shaped object. India frowned.

"It's a cat flap," her mom explained. "Ernie's coming over tomorrow to install it in the back door. It means Todd will be able to come and go whenever he likes once he's used to his new home and surroundings."

"Oh, Mom. So you *do* like him," said India.

"Of course I do," said her mom, hugging her. "Like all of us, he's just getting used to his new home. He's certainly not the little troublemaker he was."

At that very moment, Todd ran up the velvet curtains.

"Oops," gulped Mandy.

"Todd, no!" said India, unhooking his claws and bringing him down.

Mrs. Arquette was completely calm. "I think it's time to introduce the activity ball."

Todd adored his new toy. He chased it all over the dining room, stopping only to eat the treats when they fell out. After a while, he stopped playing with it and picked up James's string toy in his mouth. He dragged it over to India and looked up at her, a satin bow in his mouth.

Mandy chuckled. "I think Todd's trying to tell you something."

"And Happy Valentine's Day to you, too, Todd," said India, with a big smile.

"Now that's the sort of thing I'll miss out on," said Mr. Arquette, and added quickly, "Todd's little jokes, I mean."

"I could send you photos of him," said India.

James was crunching the last piece of the crispy bread. "I've got an even better idea."

"What?" Mandy asked. She felt something brush against her. She looked down and saw Todd curling up on her feet. She reached down and stroked the tip of his velvety ear with one finger. After racing about so energetically, he was worn out.

"A blog. Like Chad's," said James.

"What?" Dr. Adam looked confused. He turned to his wife, who shrugged her shoulders.

In contrast, Mr. Arquette seemed impressed.

"Really, you guys!" Mandy teased. "A blog's an online diary."

"Oh," said her dad, looking even more perplexed.

James was warming to his idea. "You can post updates every day, and lots of pictures of Todd so that your dad can keep up to date with his progress," he said to India. "And I bet it won't just be your dad checking out the site. When other people find it, you'll get loads of hits."

As James' enthusiasm grew, Mandy saw her mom and dad's confusion growing, too. "Never mind," she told them, and hugged her dad. "It's much more important for you to know everything about animals than anything about computers."

"I'm glad to hear that," said Dr. Adam.

"It's a good thing we're all different," said Mrs. Arquette. "Even if it means we don't always understand each other." She gave India's dad a fleeting look before picking up Todd's activity ball and putting it on a side table.

"True," said Mr. Arquette. "But the main thing is, we understand Todd now. And the next important thing is to come up with an address for your blog, India."

"That's easy," said India. "www.HaberayAlgernon Todd.com."

"Yeah, that's pretty unusual. It should be available," said James.

"Works for me," said her dad. "What do you think we should put on your homepage? You need to welcome visitors to your site so they come back again, and tell their friends!"

Mandy's parents looked more lost than ever.

"I know exactly the right picture for it," Mandy said. "Excuse me, please." She pushed back her chair and went to get the photograph.

"Right on!" said India when Mandy brought it back in.

It was the picture of Todd, curled up in his heart-shaped box, with one amber eye open to reveal a gleam of mischief. The grown-ups gave James a round of applause for his excellent photography.

"Once he's on the front page of your blog, people from all over will be able to see him. He'll be famous around the world as the kitty in the candy-heart box," Mandy declared, and she bent down to stroke the gorgeous little cat once more as he lay sleeping at her feet.

ABOUT THE AUTHOR

Ben Baglio was born in New York, and grew up in a small town in southern New Jersey. He was the only boy in a family with three sisters.

Ben spent a lot of his childhood reading. English was always his favorite subject, and after graduating from high school, he went on to study English Literature at the University of Pennsylvania. During his coursework, he was able to spend a year in Edinburgh, Scotland.

After graduation, Ben worked as a children's book editor in New York City. He also wrote his first book, which was about the Olympics in ancient Greece. Five years later, he took a job at a publishing house in England.

Ben is the author of the Dolphin Diaries series, and is perhaps most well known for the Animal Ark and Animal Ark Hauntings series. These books were originally published in England (under the pseudonym Lucy Daniels), and have since gone on to be published in the U. S., and translated into 15 languages.

Aside from writing, Ben enjoys scuba diving and swimming, music and movies. He has a beagle named Bob, who is by his side whenever he writes.

ACTION, MYSTERY, AND ADVENTURE AT EVERY TURN

DELTORA
by Emily Rodda
Enter the realm of monsters, mayhem, and magic.
www.scholastic.com/deltora

SPY X
by Peter Lerangis

Twins Andrew and Evie navigate a maze of intrigue as they try to uncover the truth about their mother's disappearance.
www.scholastic.com/spyx

GUARDIANS *of* GA'HOOLE
by Kathryn Lasky

A thrilling series about an owl world where unknown evil lurks, friends band together, and heroism reigns supreme.

www.scholastic.com/gahoole

Special Bonds with Special Friends

Paws, hoofs, or fins — Mandy is there to lend a helping hand as she rescues animals in need.

By Ben M. Baglio

Heartland

Healing horses, healing hearts...

By Lauren Brooke

Nestled in the foothills of Virginia, there's a place where horses come when they are hurt. Amy, Ty, and everyone at Heartland work together to heal the horses—and form lasting bonds that will touch your heart forever.

Chestnut Hill

By Lauren Brooke

From the author of the Heartland books comes a smart, sassy series set at an exclusive all-girls boarding school in Virginia, where horses—and winning—mean everything.

■ SCHOLASTIC

Available wherever you buy books.